YOCANDRA IN THE PARADISE OF NADA

YOCANDRA IN THE PARADISE OF NADA

a novel of cuba

ZOé VALDéS

TRANSLATED FROM THE SPANISH BY **SABINA CIENFUEGOS**

ARCADE PUBLISHING • NEW YORK

First published in France under the title *Le néant quotidien* (Spanish title, *La Nada Cotidiana*)

Arcade Publishing books may be purchased in bulk at special discounts for sales promotion, corporate gifts, fund-raising, or educational purposes. Special editions can also be created to specifications. For details, contact the Special Sales Department, Arcade Publishing, 307 West 36th Street, 11th Floor, New York, NY 10018 or arcade@skyhorsepublishing.com.

Arcade Publishing® is a registered trademark of Skyhorse Publishing, Inc.®, a Delaware corporation.

Visit our website at www.arcadepub.com.

10 9 8 7 6 5 4 3 2 1

Library of Congress Cataloging-in-Publication Data is available on file.
ISBN: 978-1-61145-933-3

Printed in the United States of America

For my daughter Attys Luna,
born in a periodo especial

"Why something rather than nothing?"

— E. M. CIORAN

CONTENTS

YOCANDRA IN THE PARADISE OF NADA

1

"Morir por la patria es vivir"

Fear of the future lessens the fear of death.

—Marguerite Yourcenar

*S*HE COMES FROM AN ISLAND *that had wanted to build paradise. The fire of aggression consumes her face. Her eyes are almost always moist, her mouth is imploring, like a bronze statue, her nose pointed.*

She is like any other woman, except that she opens her eyes in the manner of the island women: beneath her eyelids lurks quiet indifference. In stark contrast to her liquid pupils, her body is tense. She is not really beautiful, but she does have

1

something, though just what that is would be hard to say. *Perhaps it is her ironic smile. Perhaps her extraordinary fear. She never changes and never will. She will die young and with all her desires.*

"What is your name?" asks the Seraph.

She thinks she has heard an angel's voice but does not reply. The formless sea lies behind her thoughts. Suddenly she has forgotten her name. And the angel.

Her body is enveloped in darkness. Her legs refuse to respond to the mind's command to move forward. She levitates. Her legs do not exist. And she? Does she exist?

She is hungry and has nothing to eat. Her stomach knows very well that it must resist. On her island, every part of the body learned to resist. Sacrifice was the order of the day, as was nada, *nothingness. To die and to live: the same verb as to laugh, except that you laughed in order not to die from an excess of compulsory living.*

Space is transformed into a white cloud, pure and pristine. A whitewashed wall. Whatever. There is no one. Not even a spirit. No one but her. Continuing to believe she exists.

Lighter than air, and still levitating, she finds a mirror and to pass the time examines her sex. Female. No question about it. From the short scar, six stitches from vulva to anus, she understands, or is reminded, rather, that she has borne children. How many? She doesn't know. Her memory is an enormous garden of clocks. The ticktocking and chiming keep her from remembering. Ideas — strange, morbid ideas — filter through her thoughts. Ideas and feelings, rising out of nowhere. A spreading fan of images forces her to take a deep breath. She is completely drugged. She loves the taste of flight, the feel of a voyage into the void.

When she returns to herself she weeps without tears, but there is a brilliance to her expression. The salty liquid does not run down her cheeks. She sobs as she caresses her frozen hands. Just as she thinks she must go, her strength suddenly leaves her. . . . She will always have to leave, and always lose strength, lose hope . . . lose herself . . . ourselves . . . leave. . . . There will always be a place, a country waiting for us, a nada *waiting for us . . . a tender nothingness.*

A handsome blond angel arrives, also levitating, and floats beside her. When he speaks to her, his jasmine-scented breath tickles her. Makes her dream, and more. She immediately falls in love with him.

"Did you land here by accident?" the angel asks.

"Accident. I don't like that word. I landed here by chance."

"Sweet lady, chance no longer exists. Beware of all outmoded expressions. It is better to seem ignorant than nostalgic."

"What are you referring to, O exalted angel? You are an angel, are you not?"

"Of course I'm an angel. I'm referring to all creatures like you, innocent and yet guilty. Creatures conscious and unconscious. Now, dear queen, this very day."

"I am not a queen."

"You seem like one, my queen. I was saying that these days the universe is in a kind of radical dissolution. Torn

asunder. One can't be one thing and at the same time its opposite. One has to be careful."

She understands nothing the angel is saying but decides that he speaks like an infinite being: false and beautiful, inhuman and at the same time kindhearted. She reverts to what she used to be — the little girl timid in front of strangers.

No sooner has she begun to reflect upon the obscurity of her past than the angel is obliterated by a bolt of golden lightning.

She weeps, inconsolably, though still without tears. Her head slumps forward to her naked breasts. She has nothing on but feels no shame. A fragile, dying bird, she knows that her childhood is buried deep within herself, and she knows that she has not aged. She is in the middle, the exact middle, of the ages, the numbers, the inexplicable. Ahead lies mystery; behind are shadows.

We might have thought that night had fallen and the stars come out, resplendent as ever. However, it is not night, nor is there a splendid, star-studded sky. There is only silence. The deafening sound of silence. Its litany gives the impression of night.

So many sensations! The cool of the breeze, a kiss on the lips, friendship, the dense music of the forest. And a laugh. She searches in vain for a face among the foliage. No one, only a burst of raucous laughter.

"Is someone there?" She is trembling.

"Of course there's someone. You!" responds the Nothing.

Unsatisfied, she keeps pressing for an answer.

"Search no more! I exist and I do not exist!" says the Nothing.

"To whom . . . have I the honor of speaking?" she asks, putting up a brave front. "Who are you?"

"I am that I am. The one who decides," proclaims the emptiness.

She thinks that no matter where you go, there is always the "one who decides." She has never been "she who decided for herself."

"I am here to explain why you must leave."

She's not sure she wants to know why. Knowing why means tearing open old wounds.

"All right, I'll explain. We're in purgatory. You're dead. And we, They Who Decide, are faced with a serious dilemma. You see, you have fifty points toward admission to paradise, and fifty points toward being sent to hell. Your soul is too innocent to deserve hell, and just evil enough not to deserve paradise. We can't allow you to remain indefinitely in purgatory. So—"

"So?"

She has a fever. She wants to argue but can't find the strength. Her strength is fading fast.

"So I am the One Who Decides." The voice of Nothing pierces her.

A golden shaft of light strikes her eyes, her naked body, her mind, which is half at peace, half agitated. She dreams that oceans of tears pour down her cheeks. She opens her eyes in the manner of the island women. She is still naked, stretched out on the sand, the sea around her, caressing her feverish skin. They have forced her to return to her island, the island that in wanting to build paradise has created hell.

She doesn't know what to do. Why swim? Why drown?

2

My Heroic Birth

*A*CCORDING TO MY MOTHER, it was the first of May, 1959. She was nine months pregnant and already knew I was a girl. She walked and walked, she says, all the way from Old Havana to the Plaza de la Revolución to hear the Comandante. And in the middle of his speech I started to raise such a ruckus in her pelvic region that she thought her bones would break. They had to carry her out on their shoulders to the Quinta Reina clinic. Before she could make her way through the huge crowd, however, as she passed the speakers' platform, Che himself draped a

Cuban flag over her belly. She hardly noticed, because I was putting her through such hell. All the while, Fidel was going on and on with his speech, his rhetoric denser than a forest of palm trees. And I kept kicking, elbowing, butting my head, trying any which way to escape from her body.

Her belly sagged all the way down to her pubis. It felt like an explosion of constellations inside her, she says. She closed her eyes and savored the pain of expectation. My father arrived, covered from head to foot in a layer of red dirt that he was trying to dust off, his palm-leaf hat pulled down over his eyebrows, his machete still in his hand. They had gone to get him at the sugarcane harvest. He crouched next to her belly and trembled when he saw the flag. When she told him that Che himself had put it there, he almost fainted with pride. He stuck out his chest, smiled with satisfaction.

She says that at that moment she was no longer sure what she was feeling were labor pains. Maybe it was just a stomachache. But after so many contractions, she realized that it couldn't be just some minor body function. Her body was taking on a whole new dimension, alternating between the microscopic and the macroscopic. Her intimacy was exposed to its limits, like some mathematical equation. She was a step away from the flickering Void. And so much life inside! My father, a bundle of nerves, swore over and over again that he loved her. Without him she could not have faced it. She pretended to be tough.

She went into the bathroom and passed bloody, greenish stool. She spent the night whispering, over and over, "I'm going to give birth. This time I'm *really* going to give birth."

My father is forever reminding me how brave my mother was throughout her life. I was her first and only daughter. She was unaware — like every woman — how painful childbirth could be, and that unawareness made her defensive. She could never overcome her fear. They made her put on a ridiculous-looking hospital gown, short and low-necked, and had her lie down on a sweat-soaked hospital cot. They spread her legs. Now she would really find out about pain. The obstetrician ordered her to push with each contraction. He stuck his hand in, poked around, taunting her every push. The pain was like the pain of death. Life was beginning, but it felt instead like life was ending. My mother's waters hadn't broken, so they broke them with a long white plastic stick. A cascade of warm, sticky liquid spewed out, and this gave her courage. The specialist's hand shook her belly violently. There, where I am. Where I was.

They carried her over to a drab little room. Outside, my father was chewing his nails, pulling out his hair. He didn't even dare smoke. The walls of the room were gray with filth, the chairs as well, the two beds hidden behind folding screens. Every armchair held a moaning pregnant woman with bruise-covered arms hooked up to IV bottles. My mother waited with them, wasting away in a humiliating hospital gown, her belly still draped with the Cuban flag that Che had placed there.

Elena Luz, the guerrilla doctor, decided that though my mother was already dilated almost three inches, her contractions were too far apart. They hooked up an IV to her arm, which had been tanned by the sun during the demonstration and the Workers of the World Day parade. My mother said she felt like a dissected cow, as in one of those Dutch still lifes. She could no longer control the rhythm of her labor pains. Doctors came and went, prodding her belly and sticking their strange hands inside her.

She walked back and forth between the armchair and the bed. The doctors told her to push hard. She was trying not to faint. Again strangers' hands pried opened her vagina and felt around inside. Her insides were like a turtleneck. Blood flowed from her everywhere — her clitoris, her anus; she urinated, emptied her bowels. Her body was at the mercy of the blasé mediocrity she saw in the doctors' gazes.

With unseeing eyes, she gripped her knees as hard as she could and then pushed, roaring like a lioness. One leg broke free from her grasp and knocked the IV bottle to the floor. They gave her a shot in the other arm. Once more the fierce grinding inside her, the indescribable pain. According to the experts, she was about to give birth; according to her, she was about to implode. They made her walk to the delivery room. Halfway there, a great ripping tore her from vulva to anus. My head!

She climbed onto the bed in the delivery room. One push: nothing. Another tremendous, three-dimensional push. My head was stuck. Then one final push, the most powerful of all, the one that made her a mother and me a daughter. Burning. Pushed to the edge of death. In that push, she says, Life and the Great Beyond became one. "Could that be God?" She still wonders.

She wanted to watch me emerge from her body, and cried softly, like a cat purring. I was easy and slippery. I was detached from myself. I still am. My mother ceased being me. I ceased being her. They cleaned up her insides with icy water and showed her the enormous placenta, as beautiful as a piece of sculpture. It still hurt, like nothing and everything. They sewed her up carefully. She knew she was losing a lot of blood. How long would the pain of the life force go on? Cut off from her universe, I set out into my own. Her pain had ended. Mine had just begun.

My father was beside himself with joy, though he was also bitterly disappointed that I hadn't been born on May first. There I was, a tiny little lump slimy with maternal gook, wrapped in the Cuban flag, and already my father was scolding me for failing to fulfill my revolutionary duty.

"She should have been born yesterday! Two minutes! Missed by two minutes! I've been betrayed! She should have been born on the first of May! I'll never forgive either of them!" He lamented my lateness over and over again, his expression nonetheless euphoric. The doctor tried to console him:

"Don't be so upset, *compañero*. Today is also an important day. It is the Day of the Madrid Uprising, the Executions in Madrid — Goya's painting, remember?"

My father didn't know the first thing about Spanish history — or about any other history, for that matter. Maybe just a little about the war of independence against the Spaniards. The only thing he was sure of was that the Yankees were his enemy and that his Revolution had been born on January first and that his daughter had been born in the spring, which here in the tropics amounts to the same thing, because the weather is hot as hell at both times of year.

"What will you call the little girl?"

"Hmm . . . I'll call her Victoria. Better yet . . . yes, even better . . . Patria! Patria's an original name! I'll be the father of Patria! The fatherland! The father of the fatherland! Carlos Manuel de Céspedes! The first man to free his slaves! Now there was a man with balls!"

Deeply moved by his own words, my father began to sob uncontrollably, believing himself glorious.

3

Yocandra, between Terror and Shame

*T*HREE OPEN WINDOWS confirm the sea's existence. If it exists, that means I am sitting on the edge of the bed, as I do every morning, sipping bitter dark coffee that only minutes ago was powder and now is liquid. How long ago did I begin this ceremony? Sipping coffee and looking at the sea, as if each wave contained a fragment of life? Looking at the water slowly hypnotizes me and makes me feel serene. It both terrifies and soothes. Every morning for an uncountable number of dawns I've been doing the same thing, traversing the foam with the holy body, while the soul, like the sea, murmurs its existence to me. It's like vertigo. Everything is forever out of balance, inside me and outside in the world. Nothing terrifies me, yet everything tells me that terror is everywhere. There must be some extraordinary secret the gods have hidden in plain view, jolting us into believing in them, leading us into thinking ourselves the instruments of some exquisite utility. They do this to control our search for coherence, for a perfect harmony between the infinite and the ephemeral. To be human is a gift the gods conferred too hastily. And the great mystery is this: to whom shall the gift be given?

I was born choking. My head got stuck in my mother's birth canal, and because of that I will always suffer from shortness of breath. But my labored breathing allows me to palpitate with life, second by second. And in these seconds are questions — questions when I breathe in, questions when I breathe out. It's a double exercise, physical and mental. How can everyone demand strict discipline in one's responses when reality is such a cataclysmic swarm of question marks?

For how many centuries has my mouth been enjoying my morning coffee, my eyes gazing out at this sea, my legs unmoving and therefore ready to spring in every direction?

A traitor slept in my bed last night, a nihilist the night before. How long have I had this passion for alternation? Why do I continue with one when I haven't ended things with the other? Do I need to live by emphasizing the difference? Do I have to dwell on the human drama of time? Why must I think so much about the past? Is this double life really necessary, this shuttling back and forth between instinct and analysis, or vice versa, each side mistrusting the other? Why does this surge of old emotion invade my silence and make me realize I'm still breathing? Is all this just the crisis of a woman hitting her thirties?

The coffee woke me up. I have brushed my teeth and eaten my breakfast, which consisted of water sweetened with a little brown sugar and a quarter of the four ounces of yesterday's bread ration. I've become an expert at rationing my daily bread — when, that is, there is bread. I cut it into four portions: one for lunch, one for dinner, a third before I go to bed — if I haven't already shared it with someone who's come to pay me a visit — and the fourth for breakfast the following day. After breakfast, I brush my teeth again. I have some toothpaste because a neighbor traded it to me for a little *picadillo de soya*, which is something I wouldn't be caught dead eating. Foul-smelling, greenish garbage. God only knows what they put into it. They have forced me to become a vegetarian, even though there isn't much available in the way of vegetables either.

I slip into the first clean dress I can lay my hands on, tie my hair up with a clip, and take a last glance at myself in the mirror. I look pretty good. Ready for battle. I lift the bicycle out from behind the couch in the living room, check to make sure there's still some air in the tires, grab my knapsack, open the door, and descend the eight floors on foot, my Made in China bicycle slung over my shoulder. The elevator doesn't work. Even if it did, there's no electricity. I manage the steep steps in total darkness, but by the time I get to the ground floor my dress is drenched with sweat.

So now I'm in the street, pedaling away as I do every day, so lost in my thoughts that a truck could flatten me at any moment. I'm on my way to the office: *to work*. What work, you ask? For the past two years I've been doing the same thing, day in, day out. I bike from my house to the office, punch my time card, sit at my desk and read the foreign magazines — which I always get two or three months, if not two or three years, late — and then drift off into daydreams. Our literary magazine, of which I'm the editor in chief, can't be printed because of "the material problems with which our country is faced during this Special Period," and because of everything else we've had to endure and probably will go on enduring in the days and months ahead. My daydreams almost always end at lunchtime. I open my knapsack, take out the quarter portion of bread, half a banana, and drink my jar of water sweetened with the dregs from a sugar refinery. If I have any coffee left at the end of the month, it's nothing short of a miracle. The only reason I have a little left over this month is because I traded it for a piece of soap. Whoa! I just went through a red light. Still lost in my thoughts. I leave my office at two in the afternoon (nobody works until five anymore). I ride back to the house, my mind, as always, a million miles away. I'm home. No electricity. I begin cooking dinner at three in the afternoon, because the gas keeps going off and I'll be lucky if I eat by eight or nine. Most of the time I eat at midnight. While the pot languishes on the stove, I have time to take a bath. So I go down to the corner and get a couple of buckets of water, which I have to haul up the full eight flights. It takes three, sometimes four trips. I spill so much water that I often have to mop the stairs, using an old towel. Mops are precious commodities; they cost a dollar and a half at the foreign-currency market at Setenta. After dinner I clean up the apartment, then read something before going to bed, or if the power is back on, I watch a video. This is more or less my routine on those days when the Traitor or the Nihilist isn't visiting. Daydreaming means either thinking about them or, as I'm doing now, reviewing the daily facts of my existence. Yesterday, for example, I brushed my teeth before breakfast but not after, and I felt uncomfortable all day. My teeth didn't feel clean. Yet I can't eat breakfast without *first* brushing my teeth, and when I do that my breakfast has no taste, which is fine because it has no taste to begin with.

Must get across Avenida Grande before the light turns red. No way. Can't pedal fast enough. Have to pull up.

"Patria! Patria! Hey, girl! Don't you recognize me?"

I do recognize her. It's that militant nutcase from agricultural school who always used to stick me with weekend guard duty just to piss me off and keep me from meeting boys. I refuse to look over at her or to reply, but the stupid light's still red and she's coming over.

"Hey, Patria, are you deaf? Don't you remember me?"

"I've changed my name. I'm Yocandra now."

The militant nutcase looks me over suspiciously, from head to toe. "Why? Weren't you proud of your name?"

The light changes from red to yellow to green, but the militant nutcase is leaning heavily on her handlebars, her pupils boring into mine.

"I wasn't worthy of the name," I answer.

"You haven't become a *gusana*,* have you? Into human rights and all that?"

"No, I just wanted to be Yocandra. Out of love . . ."

"Love of what? Love of who? You could have kept your *old* name out of love. So anyway, if you ever run into me again, don't say hello. Okay? Times are tough, and, as you may know, I work for a French company now and it's being watched by the police. They spend all their time checking up on me. I can't afford to lose my job because— Hey, Patria! What's wrong with you? Why are you pushing me away?"

I'm pushing you away because I don't want to hear any more of your crap. I have enough of my own. Oppor-

* Literally, "worm," a name applied by Cubans to their compatriots who have fled to the U.S. or who do not believe in the Revolution. — *Tr.*

tunistic bitch! You can go straight to hell as far as I'm
concerned. You who used to report anyone you saw talking
to foreigners. How many students had their I.D. cards
confiscated; even got kicked out of school because of you?
Fascist slut! Now you're working for a foreign company?
I'm not Patria anymore because I always hated the name,
because in grade school everyone made fun of me, because
deep down I feel the most profound respect for the true
meaning of the word, and because of the first man I fell in
love with, when I was sixteen — the one I married and
divorced, before getting remarried three more times (in
the tropics we marry and divorce as easily as we drink a
glass of water).

The Traitor. After all this time, and all those husbands, he's still my lover, the one I alternate with the
Nihilist, my other lover, the young one, the man I truly
love. Sleeping with the Traitor is my revenge and my
addiction, my way of humiliating him, paying him back
for all the suffering he put me through.

Here's how it all began. When I first met him and
told him my name he burst out laughing. I can't go to bed
with the Fatherland! he shouted. I'd rather die first! That
night, as he was buttoning up my school uniform, he told
me not to come and see him again until I'd changed my
name. I was sixteen and dreamed of becoming a world-
famous writer. He was thirty-three and said he'd published two novels, three volumes of essays, and a book of
poetry. His work was much in vogue at the time. He was

handsome and dressed well. I clearly remember a spiffy Italian suit, pale-blue to match kid leather shoes that were as soft and tender as *nada* to the touch. He had curly light-brown hair. His eyes were the color of honey, and his complexion had that faint pink flush of good health. A brilliant writer. Everybody said so. He traveled a lot (I learned this during one of our first meetings, when he showed me photo albums filled with pictures from all the countries he'd visited). He spoke Italian — learned it from an Italian mistress who was older than he; and French — learned it from a Swiss man who was older than he; and Russian, which to be honest he spoke badly.

When he didn't make love to me that first night because of my name, I cried bitter tears. I was inconsolable. He pretended I didn't exist and buried himself in a fat book with a gilt cover. Years later, he admitted to me that he'd only been pretending to read. He was waiting to see how I would react. I reacted in a most unusual way. I took a manuscript from his desk: a manuscript of poetry dedicated to someone named Yocandra. Suddenly I was overcome with blind jealousy, the kind that makes you want to beat your head against the wall. But I contained myself. My burning eyes glued to each page, I read the manuscript from beginning to end. I thought it was a work of genius (today it strikes me as merely naive). How I wanted to be the woman who had inspired this noble mind with so much love and suffering! I cursed myself for not having been born, like her, in another country. I wanted to be a foreigner. I wanted to have blue eyes and hair so blond it was white, like the Swedes, and speak with an accent. I didn't want to be me. Tears spattered the skirt of my school uniform, which was mustard colored — monkey shit we used to call it. Sobbing, I put this masterpiece of Cuban literature back on his desk and, in a religious silence, went out into the growing darkness of the Havana evening.

The next day I did all the paperwork; I threatened my parents that I would drop out of school. That night I went up to the Traitor's room and knocked softly. He opened the door, stark naked. He was so tall that he had to bend down to see me.

"Why, if it isn't the Fatherland herself!" He laughed sarcastically.

"No . . . no," I stammered, trembling and timid. "I've changed my name to . . . Yocandra." In the semidarkness, his face looked purple. I had to repeat myself several times. It was as if he hadn't heard me. "Yocandra," I said. "Like the woman of your poems."

"Who gave you permission? Who the hell do you think you are, stealing the name of my muse? This is too much! For years I racked my brain, trying to find a title that publishers would find intriguing. *Poems of Yocandra's.* And then a ridiculous little twerp like you comes along and steals it! Do you know what future scholars will think when they study my work? They'll think I named the book after you. They'll think you were the inspiration for those poems! When the truth is that you stole them!"

"I'm sorry. I . . . thought you'd like me more."

"Like you more?" he roared. "You thought I'd like you more? Have you looked at yourself in the mirror? You're nothing but a spoiled, knobby-kneed little brat! And a thief! Worse, a spy! I have a lot of enemies, you know. There are people who'd like nothing better than to cast a spell on me, dry up my brain!"

"Fine, I'm leaving. I only thought that making love with you would be romantic, different, like in the novels. Don't worry. Tomorrow I'll get my old name back."

I was turning to go, when the Traitor seized me by the shoulders and began sucking the nape of my neck. No one had ever done that to me before. He took me by the hand and led me into his lair. Not from desire. Even less from love. Ah, no! Just to be perverse.

4

The Traitor

*H*OW DID I MEET THE TRAITOR? I was on my way
home from typing class, given by a woman who was always
putting on airs and acting as if she were some kind of
refined lady, even though she secretly ran a school in a
room of what had been a mansion and was now a run-
down tenement on the Calléjon del Chorro. All of a
sudden it began to rain furiously, one of those Havana
downpours with raindrops so big they hammer your skull
and thunder so loud it shatters your eardrums. The lightning flashes were blinding. Deathly afraid of lightning —

and even more of turning into a walking lightning rod —
I emptied my pockets of everything metallic and ran out
into the middle of the street to avoid being crushed by
some falling object. I began to pray as loud as I could:
"San Isidro, patron saint of water, stop the rain. Make
the sun come out again!"

There wasn't a soul in the street. Except at the far end
of the park, wrestling with a black umbrella in the howling
wind and the driving rain, there was a man, studying me as
a beast does its prey. I walked past him. He offered to share
his umbrella. My response was a stare so icy that my pupils
and tear ducts still ache. He followed me. The rainwater
had made my dress transparent, and he wanted to sink
his teeth into my firm flesh, my "sovereign skin," in the
words of the poem Lezama Lima dedicated to Fina (years
later, the Traitor told me that throughout his life, Lezama
had been in love with Fina — platonically, of course). I
was ready for his bites. And ready for his betrayals too.
He never thought of me as pretty — as he told me frequently — but considered me a victim, and that was what
he was looking for, what he's still looking for. He led me to
the shelter of a convent door and recited a passage from his
latest book, a copy of which he took from his leather
briefcase and inscribed for me. Without asking me my
name, he wrote, "To a young girl born of the rain." Night
surprised us still there, he talking about great literature, I
about the latest Soviet novels on sale at the new bookstores. In the older bookstores you could still find small

treasures. Every time I mentioned a Soviet book, he looked disgusted. When I mentioned a Cuban or Latin American book I had read, his face registered approval and he congratulated me, then planted a sloppy kiss on my forehead.

After that he began to pursue me. He stationed himself at the corner of my building to check me out, had friends find out virtually everything about me. I say "virtually everything" because he only thought he knew everything. Finally one night I went to see him at the *solar*, a pretty seedy hangout for Cuban intellectuals, painters, artisans, writers, musicians, journalists, architects, engineers, actors, and various lowlifes as well. There was one native from the southern part of the country who asked people to call him Argelino; there was a reprobate with thirty-six cats and two German shepherds (they all lived in a single room), who called himself Al Cafotano, in honor of Al Capone; then there were a pimp, a drug dealer, a guy who trafficked in foreign currency. That night the Traitor learned my name. It stunned him. And so the next day I came back with my name changed, and my life too.

That second night he asked me if I was a virgin. I told him that of course I was, and it was true. No one had ever penetrated my vagina, and my hymen was intact. He couldn't deal with that. Exasperated, he shook his finger threateningly at me and showered me with abuse. If I was a virgin, then someone would have to deflower me, and it wasn't going to be he. He simply wasn't up to it. He couldn't bear the idea of tearing open something as sensitive as a hymen! (How could he have guessed that later on he would tear to shreds things that were even more sensitive: my dignity, my soul, and all the other crap so important to women?) I would have to leave, he said, and come back only after I'd been deflowered. And God forbid that I should try to tell him how it had happened. The last thing he wanted to know were the sordid details, which could only have a negative effect on our future sexual relations.

I could have explained to him that my vagina was indeed virgin but that the other c(anal) was considerably less pure. Despite the fact that some of the girls at school tried to scare us into thinking you could get pregnant by the back door, that only one drop on your thigh could screw you up for good.

I used to wait until dark, then grope against the wall of the Castillo de la Fuerza with a fifty-year-old ex-political prisoner. He had just been let out. He told me that his only crime had been to toss a handful of stones against a window in which the 26th of July flag and a number of stupid political slogans were displayed. For that they'd given him thirteen years in jail. It was a pleasant enough experience, this back-door sex, though it hurt a little. He introduced me to a fair number of books, such as Mario Benedetti's *The Truce*.

All my father had to do was mention in passing one

day that the worst thing he could imagine befalling him and his family would be to find out that his daughter was fucking a black man. So I immediately took up with a handsome black man with green eyes, a merchant marine, of all things. Through him I learned all about the major ports of the world, especially Hamburg — in those days it was still part of the German Federal Republic — and the streets of São Paulo, world famous for its prostitutes. I finally had to ditch my emerald-eyed sailor. He was tired of being allowed in only through the service entrance and kept pressing to be admitted through the front door. At that point in my life, however, I wasn't courageous enough to say yes. Besides, I didn't have the slightest means of fending for myself financially, and I would have been forced to if my racist father ever found out.

So in reality I was a virgin only in the formal sense. But who could have dared interrupt the gesticulations of this wild man, this prisoner of his obsessions? The Traitor — tears streaming down his cheeks — opened the door. Out walked not a frightened young girl but one with a killer hymen, ready, willing, and able to murder the first penis that crossed its path. Except that of my beloved.

A long-haired guy was waiting alone at the bus stop at the Casablanca docks. He was so full of rum and pot that he had absolutely no clue where he was going. All he knew was that he had to get the hell away from the docks. I took his head and shoved it into the murky, foul-smelling waters of the Malecón, which was covered with an oily sheen. Then I planted myself in the middle of the avenue, showed a little tit, and managed to hitch a ride with an army general. I told him that my brother was having an asthma attack and I had to get him to a hospital. He dropped us off near the emergency room of Calixo García. As soon as the general's license plate was out of sight, I dragged the pathetic longhair over to The Red, a dimly lit nightclub in the center of the Vedado. It turned out that his name was Machoqui and that sometime around 1975 he had made up his mind to become a hippie, long after there were hippies in the world, let alone in Cuba. I slapped him four times, threw two pitchers of cold water on his idiotic face, and began to kiss him in order to maintain a modicum of romance. On a battered bench reeking of sweat, and to the tune of a bolero sung by José Antonio Méndez himself, he opened his fly and fished out a well-stiffened prick. I already had my panties down around my ankles. All I could think of was a guillotine. Without further ado, I sat myself down squarely on the head of his member. He was the one who let out a cry of pain; I wasn't moist enough. It took some doing, but finally I managed the beheading. It didn't hurt much, and all there was to show for it was a watery bloodstain, but my hymen had accomplished its mission: to murder a penis. When the deed was done, my beheaded victim vanished without a trace. I straightened my clothes, paid, and left. As for Machoqui, my deflowerer, I never heard from him again.

❧

I went back to the Traitor's pad. He was not expecting me; when he opened the door I could see he was half asleep — it was almost dawn — and when he yawned I could see all his dental fillings. I pushed him aside and waltzed in, then did a pirouette.

"It's done," I said, smiling ecstatically.

"What's done?" he asked, lighting a cigarette.

"I've been deflowered."

"You mean you're no longer . . ."

"A virgin. All right with you if I wash up?" The hippie's sperm was streaming down to my knees.

He didn't have a bathroom. A little dazed, he went and got some water from a plastic bucket and brought it back in a large earthenware jar. Right in front of him I washed my reddened sex, then took off and rinsed my blood-stained panties. He turned away, pretending not to look, but I could tell he was watching me like a hawk out of the corner of his eye. He lit another cigarette, still observing me from behind the thick cloud of smoke. I put on my most serious expression. All I wanted, and wanted savagely — to this day I don't know why — was for him to love me.

The Traitor deflowered my innocence, and if I'm heartless today it's entirely his fault. He was destined to violate my dreams, and he did so with consummate cruelty. It was he who lied to me, and he killed me with his lies. It was he who marked me, and now I'm covered with scars. He'll never know any of this; he wouldn't know how to deal with it. I loved him as only an adolescent can love: meekly and with my mind open to any and all folly. I took his follies too seriously. He was the first man I loved, and in a certain sense this makes him exceptional.

Thus began our love story. I spent a whole school year without once setting foot in class, but it didn't make any difference. My grades were all excellent, thanks to a teacher who had been bought off for a thousand pesos (in those days, a thousand pesos was serious money). Not only did I have good grades; I was enrolled in a teachers' college. It was the time of the famous slogan, repeated among professional circles, "Vocations don't exist. Vocation means having done your duty." Everyone, en masse, had to become a professor or a doctor, because of the country's needs. Cuba also didn't have any teachers of physical education, which was a great profession to go in for because it got you a room at Ciudad Libertad — Freedom City — though of course you had to share it with four others. You got great sports equipment: tennis shoes, a jogging outfit, ultra-cool knee socks with striped colors, plus breakfast, lunch, afternoon snack, and dinner in a first-class dining hall, not to mention a swimming pool and absolutely dreamy teachers: blond, tanned, muscular, to die for. They enrolled me in this school for another thousand pesos, paid by the Traitor, of course. He earned piles of money: 325 pesos a month, plus his author's royalties, which the government had collected but then refunded to him. It also sent the top students from other schools to train as gym teachers, even those who wanted to become psychologists, journalists, diplomats, lawyers, and scientists. The best minds in the land. They had all been politically active, or worked in the fields, or gone to rallies, or engaged in a variety of brown-nosing activities that earned them their militant stripes. If you weren't a militant, you see, there was no way you could choose the career of your dreams. And anyway, the career of your dreams could easily turn into a nightmare, at least once the slogan "done your duty" was imposed, because the whole notion of "vocation" was still considered a Yankee invention and the worst kind of enemy propaganda. Pepe Soto had wanted to be a singer, and they made him into a runner — even worse, a hurdler. Julia León had dreamed of becoming a prosecutor. How many people did she later turn in to the authorities, just to prove to them that if they'd only given her half a chance, she'd have become a first-class prosecutor? Instead Julia was forced to go into medicine, specializing in gynecology and obstetrics. Today how many innocent people is she sentencing to death, I wonder?

So I missed the entire school year. I didn't go to a single physical education class. I wasn't made a militant because I used to sneak out of my room at dawn to sleep with some boy in his dorm room, and also because I refused to sleep with the secretary-general of my Communist Youth group. I was the worst in the bunch. Yet there I was — enrolled in the university. All because of the benevolence of the Traitor.

Beginning that second night, after I had met the requirements specified by the Traitor before he would make love to me, he somehow got it into his head that I was an innocent, shy young thing he had to protect from the horrors of the outside world and form in his own image. I quit my typing course. The would-be socialite typing teacher had taken my parents for a ride. After six months of banging away at the old Remington typewriter, I still hadn't learned to type using all ten fingers. One day the Traitor took off all my clothes and sat me down, naked as the day I was born, in front of his splendid Olympia. He covered the keyboard with a white cloth, then blindfolded me and began caressing my neck, my back, my buttocks, my nipples, and my navel, while he recited poems to me from the collection *En la calzada de Jesús del Monte — On Jesús del Monte Street.* I was sweating profusely, but his long, dry hands stemmed the trickles of perspiration that streamed from my neck to my nipples, from my back to the crack of my ass, from my armpits to my thighs. By nightfall I was typing 120 words a minute. No joke. That's how this militant love story begins; he ordered and I obeyed. When he was writing an essay on silent film, I screened every film, one by one, from the earliest days of the pioneering Lumière brothers right up to the advent of the talkies. I arrived with all my documentation, which I carefully set down to the right of the typewriter, and he ended up writing a brilliant essay, worthy of being included in an anthology celebrating the centenary of the cinema. When he decided to write about Gothic art, I read every art book on the subject, marking significant passages with different-colored pieces of paper, on which I carefully noted the names of both the paintings and the painters. Then I pasted corresponding tags at the tops of the relevant pages, so that he could immediately find the reproductions he wanted. Only much later did I realize (after I'd learned enough) what a complete tyrant he was, but it was he who gave me my college education — despite everything he put me through, despite all those sleepless nights, despite all the exploitation. Is that what it was? Yes, it was exploitation. I didn't realize it at the time. I followed his every order out of love. That was the way you loved, I thought. That *was* love. He, on the other hand, was acting out of enlightened self-interest. I was the student being given room and board, not to mention sex, plus a truly grand, and in his view world-class, education. Before long I had learned how to hold a fork and knife properly, the way the French do — and chopsticks too. Until then I had eaten everything with a spoon. My education was far different from that of most silly, empty-headed schoolgirls. My other duties included washing and ironing his clothes, as well as the sheets, and general housecleaning. Months later, when I finally set foot in Ciudad Libertad, I realized that what they were teaching there had nothing to do with knowledge. I fell asleep in class. I also couldn't stand the endless workouts. (I'll never grace the Olympics with my presence, I thought to myself. All I'll do is teach phys ed to children and teenagers, or, in the best of all possible worlds, to bored young nymphomaniacs like myself.) The abdominal exercises — "One-one, two-two, three-three, four-four" — the chin-ups on the horizontal bar — "One, two, three, four, and over again once more" — the deep knee-bends — "One-two-three-four. Okay, everybody! Take a break!" Three weeks, and I threw in the towel. I never went back. Yet on the wall of my parents' house, proudly and prominently displayed, hangs a diploma attesting to the fact that I'm a university graduate in physical education. The Traitor's money, once again. I've never practiced "my brilliant career." I remember when I saw that film. It moved me so profoundly that when I left the theater I told myself that if I ever had a child with the Traitor, and it was a girl, I'd name her Sybylla, after the heroine. But the very thought of children was anathema to the Traitor. When I told him what I'd been thinking, he appeared the next day with a half-dead newborn kitten, which he promptly baptized Sybylla.

Meanwhile, what were my parents thinking about all this? What were they saying? Not a thing. Because they didn't know anything about it. The Traitor and I had concocted a perfect scenario, and his good relations with the bureaucrats in various divisions of the government helped him obtain the documents necessary to back it up. As far as my parents knew, I had just finished my last year of high school on the Isle of Pines, at an exclusive boarding school that accepted only privileged kids. We told them I had been selected because of my brains and my excellent attitude, but above all because of my father's status as a union leader. As far as my parents knew, I was a true militant (which I could prove by showing my counterfeit Communist Youth membership card). As far as my parents knew, I was a student at the College of Physical Education, lived at Ciudad Libertad, and spent my vacations working in the fields, helping to fill the agricultural quotas. To my father, I was a model daughter. The Traitor was my senior professor, who paid them monthly visits to keep them abreast of their daughter's progress and her prodigious accomplishments at school. I was a top student, he said. At the head of my class. This sent my father into orgasmic paroxysms of paternal pride.

In reality, I was a prisoner in a convent: love was my religion, and the Traitor my god. In reality, I was happy, because the life I was living wasn't degrading. Besides, I had no way of judging other forms of happiness. The world outside was so ugly that I saw that room crammed with books as my treasure-filled palace. The Traitor slept all day and worked all night. Once or twice a week he went to what he called "the office," a place off limits to me. I was not allowed to trespass beyond the boundaries of this room, not even to venture out as far as Old Havana. The

Traitor belonged to me between Monserrat and the bay. Beyond those limits, he answered to no one: it was the world of his other women, his friends, "the office." When he traveled abroad, I knew he was back only when he showed up on the doorstep, wearing his pale-blue Italian suit, smoking a cigarette, his head enveloped in his eternal wreath of smoke. His suitcase was always filled with new, handsomely bound books and with presents for his family and me. As time went on, there were fewer and fewer presents for me.

The Traitor was invited to lots of official receptions: one in honor of García Márquez, another for Régis Debray, the French journalist and former cabinet member — who at the time was still left-wing and therefore popular in Cuba. Then there was a dinner with Alejo Carpentier and his wife, Lilia, and a festival for Socialist filmmakers. An endless round of ridiculous events that more and more frequently he felt he should attend. My job was deciding what clothes he should wear. The guayabera? The guayabera was supposed to be the national costume, but I always thought of it as low-rent — the uniform of the unimaginative and the opportunists. From the closet with its mirrored doors I would choose some French shirts, French cologne, an English suit, and a pair of Italian shoes. He disapproved of my choices. He said that it would be wrong to call attention to oneself with such an ostentatious display of sartorial elegance and it would be better to wear the guayabera, the one made in Mexico (the homegrown versions were outrageously bad). I never did see him decked out in those attention-getting clothes. He kept them for his trips abroad. I ironed the guayabera and the blue jeans — also made in Mexico — polished his Texan boots, sprayed him with toilet water, combed his curly locks, then sent him on his way with a kiss, which he did his best to dodge, like a woman afraid her mascara will smear. He disappeared through the ferns in the hallway, after which I would hear the creak of the iron gate opening downstairs. And I was left alone with my Proust and my Baudelaire.

One day three years later, I went over to Ciudad Libertad to bribe an assistant professor into letting me into his class, and as I was leaving, I saw that from an old Anchar (a popular and inexpensive rental car in the fifties, which in later days could be had only by paying in dollars) a masculine hand was urgently signaling me over. I was about to ignore it, when the car door swung open. My heart stopped. The Traitor! I couldn't believe my eyes. I had never seen him outside our prescribed territorial limits. I thought he had made a mistake, and even though he was calling me, I kept walking. He ran after me and grabbed my arm.

"We should get married," he told me breathlessly. "Today. Right now. I've made all the arrangements. In fact, we have to get married. I need a wife. What I'm saying is I need a 'female comrade.' I've been given an important job in Europe, and I want to be married when I go."

He pushed me into the car. As we headed for the city, my head was spinning. When we got to the Palace of Weddings, a photographer was waiting, along with two witnesses he had dragooned into service — reeking winos, pillars of the Arab Bar around the corner. The marriage lawyer was about to recite the Family Code, when the Traitor pulled a hundred pesos from his pocket. She quickly closed the book and asked, without a trace of sincerity:

"Do you take each other to be your spouse?"

"We do," said the Traitor.

I didn't reply. Two minutes went by. Three. Four. Five. I was paralyzed by anxiety. My eyes filled with tears. I thought I was going to throw up. My mother wasn't there. My father would commit suicide the minute he heard I was married (although I seemed to remember that the Party strongly disapproved of its members committing suicide). And me? I was a dead mosquito for having the gall to get married without a proper ceremony and without invitations and then getting whisked away to foreign shores. The Traitor pinched my cheek.

"What's the matter with you? Why won't you answer? I thought you would be thrilled by the idea."

The marriage lawyer began to have her doubts, in spite of the hundred pesos, and asked to see my ID card again. She verified that I was over nineteen and therefore of age. "Comrade Lawyer, listen," I wanted to say to this stranger. "I was a minor when I met him. I've spent three years in jail. I am an adult and I know what I'm doing, but what I'm doing is whatever he tells me to do, because he's a man of the world and knows what he's doing. He knows where he's going, and I'm behind him. That's why I'm his fiancée, or mistress, or secretary, or maid — oops, sorry! — I mean Comrade Who Works in His House. You see, I forgot there haven't been any maids since the Triumph of the Revolution, and —"

"Yes. I take him for my spouse."

And so I got married at the Palace of Weddings. There was no wedding dress, there were no toasts. But there were photos. Mama and Papa weren't there. But there were photos — of me looking disheveled, sweaty, and shabbily dressed. All that matters is that piece of paper on which it states in black and white that this writer and future diplomat is now the proud owner of a wife — what am I saying? — a "comrade," a *compañera!* The photographs are proof positive of our marital bliss, even though I look for all the world like a victim out of some horror film. It would have been hard to look any worse. Like Mia Farrow in that movie, the one where she's blind and they've killed off all the members of the family and she's alone with the murderer.

"From now on you have to go with me to every reception," the Traitor ordered. "We have to buy you clothes and high heels. I like it when you wear high heels — they bring out the best in you. I've always been turned on when other men ogle the women I'm with. When no one looks at them, I lose interest."

As we left the Palace of Weddings, we got our first postmarital greeting, from a couple of kids driving by in a taxi.

"Hey, good-looking! Why you shacking up with that old man? Why don't you hook up with someone your own age?"

The Traitor gave a wry smile and lit a cigarette.

"I can see we're off to a great beginning," he said.

I cut my hair very short and began to wear makeup. The Traitor started buying me outfits. My parents seemed delighted that I'd married my senior professor, though Mama locked herself in the bathroom and cried her heart out. I could hear her sobbing behind the closed door. She had dreamed of seeing me in a long white gown, everyone she knew in attendance, a wedding cake with the little porcelain figures of bride and groom on top. She had dreamed of tossing rice at the newlyweds (the monthly rations precluded more than a handful) and all those other silly, stupid things mothers think of when it comes to their daughters' weddings.

Papa held his anger in check. If the Traitor hadn't been there, he would have hauled off and slapped me hard across the face. He couldn't bring himself to do that in front of this professor, this diplomat-to-be, who had been irreproachable with the family and who was now his son-in-law. I made my appearance as a member in good standing in the high society of tropical socialism, paraded about on the arm of a famous man. I was completely snubbed by one and all. They all wondered who this creature was, wearing too much makeup and tottering around on high heels.

Whenever the Traitor was introduced to some VIP, he would swell with pride and say:

"Delighted to meet you. I'm a philosopher."

My ingenuousness — my ignorance, if you will — couldn't keep me from blushing with shame every time I heard him make this dubious and childish claim. In Cuba, there are boxers, baseball players, heroes of the sugarcane harvest, builders, doctors, poets, educators, art critics, movie critics. But philosophers? I can imagine philosophers in countries like Germany. But not in Cuba. It's too hot, and there's too much hunger. There are too many Protect and Preserve the Revolution meetings, and too many meetings to plan for other meetings, too many rallies, too many general assemblies and popular assemblies, where they argue for hours and hours about why bread doesn't get delivered on time, if it gets delivered at all. In Cuba, there is no dignity — how can you have any dignity without deodorant? — no sweet potatoes, and no tenderness. A philosopher? Living in a virtual pigsty, and without either a kitchen or a bathroom? A philosopher? Forced to carry buckets of water up to his apartment? (Actually, I was the one who carried the buckets.) Still, he insists he's a philosopher, and that's all there is to it. So what if he's never written a word of philosophy? He says he thinks a lot and that men who think are philosophers, and that someday he'll write down all those thoughts forever crowding his brain — though that's a word he dislikes intensely. He says it's completely unpoetic.

At first I blushed but I believed him. I trembled with emotion. How wonderful it was to be married to a philosopher! Even today the Traitor introduces himself as a philosopher, and he still hasn't written a line on the subject. The other day, when he was standing in line to buy some fish, the Traitor tried to push his way to the front. A fat lady slapped him so hard across the face she sent him flying into the gutter. He ended up waiting in line for six hours, reading some book by Jacques Derrida. Where in the world would anyone claim to be a philosopher? What's the point? To do nothing but think? Or daydream, like me? Maybe I'm a philosopher too, and I never even knew it.

The Traitor was not content merely to call himself a man of thought. He also described himself as a man of action, a communist Rambo, a Leninist macho man, a real tough guy who joined the underground as a messenger boy when he was only eight years old. At eleven, he was teaching peasants in the depths of the Sierra Maestra how to read and write. At fourteen, he almost lost his life in the Escambray Mountains, nearly becoming a young martyr to the cause of the Revolution — any hospital in the land would have been proud to bear his name — in a battle against counterrevolutionaries. Since then, of course, he had done his military service and participated in every sugarcane harvest. (Though his hands are as pink as a pianist's; not a callus anywhere in sight. Whereas, after no more than six seasons of working in the sugarcane harvests, I have calluses on both my hands and feet.) He had also covered the bombing of Nicaragua and Angola as a journalist and claimed to have been a secret service agent sent out on "delicate missions." My girlfriend, the Gusana, called him "the red missionary." All this did not prevent half the female population of Havana from falling at his feet. Like all men of action, the Traitor was first and foremost a womanizer. I couldn't have cared less about all these so-called heroics, and I didn't believe a word of his endless stories. I listened to them the way you listen to the two o'clock news on the radio — half asleep, punch-drunk with daily life. I wasn't in love with the hero. I was in love, I thought, with the writer and with the man. How could I ever love a pervert who could ejaculate only when the head of his penis had battered my sex into bloody submission? That was why I began masturbating. It was the only way I could sneak an orgasm with an imaginary lover. I invented him out of nothing.

For four years we lived in a foreign country. This was the first time I had left my island, and those four years could serve as the subject for a whole other novel. Someday I must write it. In the plane, I sobbed my heart out.

Playing the part of the poetess Avellaneda, I recited under my breath, while the island slipped from sight:

Pearl of the Sea! Star of the West!
Cuba the beautiful! Your resplendent sky
Spreads across the night with its veil on high,
Like the pain spreading in my saddened breast.
I am leaving! . . . leaving the people I love best.

I repeated the poem over and over, like a credo muttered before an altar, until the earth disappeared, leaving only clouds and, then, nothing. An oblivion of boredom sent me to sleep. This sleep — so deep! — lasted for the four years I spent in that far-off country — a European country, to be precise — where I was transformed into the devoted wife. For four long years I played the role of Sleeping Homely, the mistreated woman cast adrift, forever waiting for the words that would break the spell and bring her back to life.

The Traitor spent these four years locked away in an attic, writing a novel that he said would leave Nobel Prize winners in the dust. When it was completed, it would combine the Gothic hermeneutics of Umberto Eco, the philosophical depth of Marguerite Yourcenar and Thomas Mann, the powerful emanations of Patrick Süskind's *Perfume*, the poetic density of Hermann Broch, the arid rigor of Samuel Beckett, and of course the *cubanía* of Lezama

Lima and Carpentier. This masterpiece he was constructing was a collage of every author who had recently appeared
in the *Literary Weekly*. He wouldn't allow anyone to read a
single line of what he had written, however. Whenever
someone dropped by, he frantically gathered up all the
papers strewn across his desk — which was made of the
best-quality mahogany Honduras had to offer and was
purchased at Roche-Bobois — and locked them away.
When he went out, which he did rarely, he locked his
manuscript up in a safe. I began to grow suspicious.

The Traitor slept only when I wasn't in the apartment, and he was always trying to get rid of me, telling me
I should go to a museum, or to the movies, or to see some
girlfriend, or to read in a park. These outings had to be
paid for out of my meager monthly allowance. I left at
eight A.M. and came back at one in the morning, cold,
hungry, and homesick. I also came back with something
worse, or better, or in any case overwhelming: I came back
with doubt. How long could this go on? In films, in books,
in real-life homes, in other people's lives, this was not the
way love was supposed to be.

One afternoon I arrived home unexpectedly. He was
taking a shower. In three bounds I was at the door of his
study, which was unlocked, because he hadn't heard anyone come in. I leafed through the manuscript of his masterpiece, all three hundred pages of it. Every page was
filled with a single sentence: "Everyone is after me. I can't
write because everyone is after me."

The same sentence, repeated over and over again, ad nauseam, beginning on page one and continuing all the way to page three hundred. I heard the sound of the shower being turned off, and with three quick strides I was out in the stairwell. I even had time to lock the door silently behind me. Outside in the street it was snowing, and I was cold — Christ, was I cold! You son of a bitch! All this time I had been starving to death, my ovaries killing me, my stomach too, from having to shit under bridges and eat baguettes all day long (baguettes used to be cheap; I hear they're expensive now). You get tired of eating nothing but bread, however good it is, a cappella, morning, noon, and night. (I'd have offered my ass for a plate of black beans, but "back there" — in Cuba — there aren't any black beans either. When, oh, when, will they have everything they ought to have "back there"?)

What I should have done was walk straight over to the American Embassy and seek asylum — not political, marital. I started sleeping in the subway. I went from house to house. People got so fed up with me that when they saw me coming they would say, "Here comes that poor homeless woman again." We had run out of things to say to each other. I drifted from movie theater to movie theater (I even went to porno films), from museum to museum stuffed to the rafters with sculptures, paintings, catalogues, posters, postcards, photographs — all of them costing money, more money, lots of money — and to no one could I turn to say that Gustave Moreau was the painter who had most screwed up my life (one of the main ones anyway). I was the biggest *comemierda* of the century for having convinced myself that my sacrifices had been contributing to the birth of a great work by a Cuban writer who also happened to be my husband. He still is my husband, because I feel compelled to mention that whenever I am about to leave in the morning, when I am almost out the door, bathed and perfumed, a hat perched smartly on my coiffed head, my clothes clean and freshly pressed, my coat impeccably brushed clean of all lint — that's when he gets so aroused that he has to take me, fully dressed, on the white bedspread full of fluff, or on a carpet that's filthy because, filthy or not, he's not about to spend a penny on a can of carpet cleaner. Nor am I, of course, because as the "accompanying wife" I earn only sixty dollars a month and don't have the right to take an outside job. When this happens — when he gets his sudden morning urge — I have to undress, bathe all over again, insert a capsule into my vagina (he claims to have had sex with a Venezuelan woman from UNESCO who infected him with a violent dose of trichomoniasis). Don't lose your cool, I tell myself. Spray the perfume on again. Reapply your lipstick. And just when it seems that at long last I'm about to go out into the icy blasts of morning air, he sidles over and says, with gentle tenderness:

"My love, did you remember to make my lunch?"

Of course, sweetie, darling, honey pie, sugarplum, my treasure, etc. Of course I've prepared your lunch, the lunch you'll wolf down without so much as a passing thought of me, not to mention remembering to leave me some leftovers. You'll also wolf down your dinner, licking your fingers and leaving not so much as a crumb for your true love. You will, however, remember to leave the dishes piled in the sink, coffee stains everywhere, ashtrays overflowing.

Down in the street, I remember, in *The Shining*, the Jack Nicholson character writing the same sentence over and over again. "All work and no play makes Jack a dull boy." That's how this would end. I would be trapped in the labyrinth, running for my life, crying my heart out, waiting for an ax through the bathroom door or a knife in the back. *No!* A *No* as big as any *¡No!* in any Latin American election. I can't go on with this lunatic. He's driving me crazy. Driving me? I've already gone crazy!

I went back to the apartment and leveled with him. I told him I had read his novel.

"A work of genius, no?" he replied Socratically, phrasing his answer as a question.

While I packed my suitcases, he was threatening suicide. I went into the kitchen and, without saying a word, picked up a knife and handed it to him. He went on lamenting his fate. I went to the medicine cabinet and prepared a dose of cyanide. He was still moaning and groaning. The next-to-last thing I heard was:

"It's all your fault I can't write. I can feel you spying on me, and that inhibits me. Everyone's spying on me, but you do it more than anyone. *You're* the guilty one! *You're* the one to blame!"

It was all I could do to keep from laughing in his face, because I remembered the rest of the bolero's lyrics:

> You're the one to blame
> To blame for all my sorrows,
> To blame for all my problems. . . .
> You're the one who filled my life
> With sweet concerns and cares
> And bitter disappointments.

The Traitor ran to me and thrust the knife, which was razor-sharp, into my hands. He pulled open the top of his puce pajamas, fell to his knees, and begged:

"Kill me! Go ahead, kill me! Do it!"

No way, I thought to myself. I could just see the headlines in the papers and on the news:

TALENTED CUBAN WRITER MURDERED BY
GOOD-FOR-NOTHING TRAMP-WIFE WHO WAN-
DERED THE STREETS WHILE HE DEVOTED
HIMSELF TIRELESSLY TO WRITING HIS FINAL
NOVEL, DOUBTLESS A WORK OF GENIUS

I rushed around collecting my possessions, forgetting things I would really need and picking up useless stuff, so caught up was I in the throes of this soap opera straight out of the most vulgar Venezuelan tabloid.

I thought it would be the easiest thing in the world for him to forget me. Once, years before, we were having lunch in a Havana restaurant with a French name — La Fayette, I think — when he told me he never had any trouble erasing the memory of a woman. All he had to do was think of some physical defect. I have more than my share of physical defects.

The plane home, the divorce. I fell in love a second time. I got married and was widowed in the short span of two years. Yes, that's right. I'm also a young widow. I lost my second husband in an airplane accident. That could be a whole other book of love, but one I doubt I'll ever write. Why can't we write about all of life, every facet? Why does sorrow always follow sorrow, latent and profound? What if I could write that love story? It was a long time before I fell in love again, but I did finally. Did I leave my sorrow behind? No, I simply developed a genius for falling in love. I'm no longer that emotional young thing, full of fire. Now I spend my time daydreaming, or going to the Malecón and selling dresses I no longer need to the street hustlers, the *jineteras*, in exchange for dollars, or exchanging sugar for sweet potatoes, sweet potatoes for beans, beans for onions, onions for rice, rice for powdered milk, powdered milk for detergent, detergent for aspirin, aspirin for sugar — and so on and so forth — in the black market or the red market, where hardened criminals rub shoulders with the wretched of the world, the poor who for obvious human reasons cannot survive without resorting to crime. I know this sounds like the refrain of some Pablo Milanés song.

As for the Traitor, he too eventually came back to his native land and remarried a number of times. His wives always left him, because he accused them all of being spies. He goes on writing books that never get published, because he has to wait for countries with guilty consciences to supply us with paper and with electricity to run the presses. And even if we had paper and electricity, who in his right mind would publish a five-hundred-page book in which the same sentence is repeated over and over again?

One morning many years later — it was a Sunday — the Traitor knocked at my door. He was carrying a wilted orchid.

"Here," he said. "This is for you. A cattleya. To be precise," he added, playing Proust, "a mountain orchid."

I was alone. And I wanted to save this fading flower. And he looked pathetic — thin and bent and bald, his teeth stained and loose. And I knew very well — I had just looked at myself in the mirror — that I was glowing with the full radiant bloom of my thirty years. And — why not? — I let him in.

5

The House of the Ex-Cultures

I HAVE COME TO THE CONCLUSION that the most important act of my life is waking up. Waking up from the lethargy imposed by the weight of reality. Waking up each morning and drinking a cup of coffee while confirming that the sea is indeed still there, and caressing it with my eyes through the blinds of my hexagonal refuge. Waking up and drinking a cup of coffee and gazing out at the sea — such are my greatest aspirations. Will the sea never leave? Why, instead of receding, does it grow larger, over-flowing the walls of the jetty, inundating the houses, wash-ing away objects and lives? What sin has a people committed that causes the sea to demand expiation? Why doesn't it go away, leaving room for an immense garden, overflowing with flowers, a place where children can play, a place for young and old alike, a place everyone can enjoy? The sea has been in a foul mood lately, and because of this my neighbor Hernia was put in an asylum for crazies, homeless, and cripples. Hernia, you see, had lived on the ground floor, and when the hurricane of the century hit, the sea roared into her house, flooding it to the ceiling and taking her furniture, her American stove, her Russian washing machine, her Japanese fans, her Cuban refrigera-tor, the mattresses she bought in El Encanto market when she got married in 1952, the velvet-covered easy chairs, and the color television (meaning she can no longer watch *Felicidad*, the Brazilian soap opera, which was shown on Mondays, Wednesdays, and Fridays — when the electric-ity was working). She also lost her canaries, for though she managed to climb up to the second floor, clutching her dog, no one was willing to help her carry up the fifteen birdcages. People were all too busy trying to save whatever they could of their own possessions. The problem was that the sea had arrived without warning. Hernia cries now. She no longer looks at the sea the way I do. She curses it, stares at it, furious with the goddess Yemayá. There are times when she wants to make peace with the sea and sends forth an offering, begging it not to come back, and she supplicates the gods as well, in the hope that they will intervene with the government, which has promised at the very least to sell her some new mattresses, though they require that she turn in the old ones, soaked with salt water as they were, as proof that her house really had been flooded and she wasn't simply making the whole story up and planning to sell the new mattresses on the black market. But the sea is indifferent, and washed away everything.

"Comrade," they insist, "if you don't bring in the old mattresses, we can't give you new ones."

Hernia doesn't have the old mattresses. The sea devoured them. And even if she did have them, she would have no way of getting them over to the place where you register as a victim of the storm in order to buy new mattresses when they do arrive — the new mattresses haven't arrived, of course; even if they had, they'd be singles, not doubles — but only if you can prove your old ones have been washed away by the hurricane.

You may well ask why this good woman spends so much time and effort over two miserable mattresses? Why doesn't she simply go out and buy two new mattresses with her own money and be done with it? Because here there are no stores that take local currency and at the Salon, which accepts only foreign currency, and caters only to foreigners, mattresses are very expensive — around five hundred bucks. And when the choice is between eggs and milk (meaning food) on the one hand and mattresses on the other, Hernia chooses food. She has no intention of using the little her family in Miami sends her to buy mattresses. Anyway, she'd have to wait a hundred years to save up enough money. So she lies on the bare floor and, because she can't sleep, stares up at the marks the sea made on the walls and ceiling. Of all the tranquilizers her psychiatrist has prescribed, not a single one is available anywhere in Cuba. This is why she has no desire anymore to listen to the homages that people pay to the sea and to other things as well. She is, as her name says, a hernia, a rupture in the neighborhood and in society.

The smallest tasks have become a complete waste of time for me. I spend ages standing in front of the mirror, my mouth filled with toothpaste (I traded some green peas to get it). What used to take me a few seconds now takes me hours, yet I still feel I've made good use of my time. That's why I feel more sure of myself, feel that I haven't lost anything. By nine A.M. I am already in the office, reading through the same articles I edited years ago, articles the authors themselves have long since forgotten they ever wrote. Calmly, meticulously, I let my mind wander and spend a good part of the morning lost in my thoughts. At noon sharp, I'll open my little package and take out my humiliating less-than-piping-hot lunch and spend an hour dreaming again about the food advertisements I see on the American television channels. My neighbor bought a satellite dish — paying a private party in dollars — that picks up everything the satellite has to offer, and just below the dish he hooked up a highly sophisticated little gadget that defies any and all governmental attempts to scramble the incoming signals. Muhammed himself couldn't prevent my neighbor from watching American television, which, crappy though it is, does show feature films and does have ads about food and deodorants and shampoos. After he got his contraption working, my neighbor hooked it up to my television, so that I could take advantage of it too. But it didn't come free. You see, my neighbor had a small problem. None of his windows faced the big satellite dish on the roof of the Hotel Habana Guitart Libre. (Free? It used to be called the Habana Hilton before the Revolution, then Habana Libre — Free Havana — after the Revolution, and now the Spaniards have bought it — in these neocolonial times? — and it is called the Guitart.) For that reason (his lacking a window facing in the right direction), he asked me — no, begged me — to let him use mine. In exchange, he told me, he would hook his system up to my TV set.

I have nothing to do. Today I could go to the beach. No one would even know I was gone. What beach? By bike? Under a sun so strong it would shrivel your papayas? (Ah, papayas! How well I remember you. You who can no longer be savored anywhere but in a work of literature!) Or I could go visit a friend and fool around and try to shake this feeling of solitude. But I already know what we'd talk about. We'd talk about the Situation. Followed by an attempt to define just what the Situation is. Then we would talk about world events, in order to transfer our problems and shortcomings to other countries (more reasons for the Situation), preferably those of the Eastern bloc. (Because today it is no longer the capitalism of the capitalistic countries we fear but capitalism as practiced by the former Communist countries.) Maybe I'll just open a book and read. But what book can I read that won't make me more miserable than I already am? Why should I try to run away from my misery? After considering all the choices, I'll end up remaining in my hexagonal refuge and, in the depths of the night, when I look with utter disgust at my pale skin, regretting that I wasted such a wonderfully sun-drenched day. (If I decide to spend the evening with some friends, I'll go to bed regretting that I wasted my time going over the same old litany of complaints.) And I'll realize that it has grown dark and that I have been leafing aimlessly through the pages of a book without reading a single word. If I do go to the beach, I'll come back dead tired and charred to a crisp and not have so much as a drop of vinegar to relieve my sunburn. There isn't even any vinegar for salad. But then there's no salad either. Who remembers salads? What I would most like is that the day not end, that night not fall, that the visible sign of time passing, the luminous dial of the battery-operated alarm clock, not frighten me so. Anyway, now that I think of it, I'm supposed to spend the evening with the Nihilist.

"Yocandra, Yocandra, wake up."

It's Rita, the secretary with the serious foot problems, gotten from harvesting potatoes without proper boots. Ten years ago they prescribed orthopedic shoes, and she sent away to East Germany to get them. Then the Berlin Wall came down. She was reduced to wearing plastic sandals. These have helped a little.

"I'm wide awake. I was just thinking about the cover of the next issue of the magazine."

She looks at me strangely and painfully, her eyes wide with her decade-long suffering, and replies with compassion:

"Honey, what are you talking about?"

For the life of me, I could never figure out why she came to the office each day.

"The . . . the cover of our magazine."

"Oh, right. I'd completely forgotten about that! Listen, the reason I came to see you was that the girl who used to work at the computer — you remember her? — the one who took a leave of absence because she lives somewhere out in the boondocks and she couldn't get a bicycle? Now you remember who she is? Good. Anyway, she's downstairs right now, selling eggs and homemade cheese. Do you want any? If so, we'd better hurry because she's leaving, and I don't have to tell you, with my foot problem and those fourteen floors, with no elevator. . . . So are you interested or not?"

"Oh, yes, my love!"

Oh, yes, my angel, my guardian angel, my sweet companion. Don't ever leave me. Stay with me always. No matter how much they cost, these eggs and cheese! A little cheese omelet tonight for dinner is a dish fit for the gods. The Nihilist said he'd bring dinner with him, but you never know. Rita is not only my secretary, she's my savior. She's in charge of "procuring" — a key word here in Cuba — everything to be had in the way of food. When it comes to food, Rita is my mother. Although in all fairness, my mother does what she can to help too, whenever her memory permits.

My poor mother. In her neighborhood, they used to call her Elsa. Now they call her "Elsewhere." She's taken refuge in the past. She's no longer here. She lives in the past tense. "Elsewhere" dreams of my birth and goes on and on about my childhood. When I visit her, she takes my head in her hands and thrusts it against her bosom, then sings to me to sleep while she rocks back and forth in her chair:

> Little tree,
> Little Christmas tree
> Bedecked all with bells. . . .
> Shepherds and kings,
> They come from afar,
> Bearing incense and myrrh,
> Following a star. . . .

She gets up and tiptoes into the kitchen. To prepare my bottle, she says. It's almost time for my three o'clock feeding. Yes, Mama has gone and won't be coming back.

On the other hand, her memory of the past — her "rage against the past," as they used to call it at school — is incredible. She remembers the strict minimum, reads aloud, like the *lector* at a cigar factory, and misunderstands everything, or rather gets everything all mixed up. For example, she calls the building where she and my father lived when I was born the Tower of Babel. It's true the building used to be filled with all sorts of distinguished people: the Jewish cloth merchants; the Asturian owners of the El Anon ice cream parlors in Muralla Street; green-grocers from Galicia; French pastry chefs; Irish butchers; Chinese cleaners and restaurant owners. Over the years, the blacks moved in too, all of them *bandoleros* — hoods and gangsters — except the ones who for generations have been the building superintendents — all as honest as the day is long, and many of whom became primary school teachers. Later, in moved the Soviets with their underarm odor, an odor that is like no other in the world.

My father had become one of the top-ranked sugar-cane cutters in the nation. One night someone knocked at the door. My father was already in his pajamas and listening to a political speech on the radio — the same speech you heard every July 26. Mama was in the kitchen, doing the dishes, humming a tune by Juan and Junior, as she listened to the only half-decent music program on the radio in those days:

Almost as gray as the winter sea . . .

What was I doing that night? If I remember, I was doing my third-grade homework, or at least pretending to. My father opened the door, and in walked a comrade with a broad smile on his face, a signal that he was the bearer of good news. He went over and embraced Papa and, with tears in his eyes, handed him two keys. Papa understood. He opened a bottle of rum. In a state of complete euphoria, he filled four glasses, so that we could all toast the happy occasion. It was the first time I had ever tasted alcohol. Mama, who was still living in the present then, felt such joy she couldn't speak.

"Finally! A new house! Thank the Lord! The Virgin too! My daughter, my Patria, you will have a room all to yourself! And we can celebrate birthdays, and you can invite lots of children to the house! So what if the car is Soviet-made. That doesn't matter! We can take you, Patria sweetheart, to the beach and to the zoo. We'll drive you all the way to Santiago de Cuba!"

Papa was overcome with emotion. Looking deep into my eyes — the last time he ever did — he gave his Patria a kiss. Because Patria was still my name.

Suddenly I got an attack of hiccups and buried my head in my arms on the table. Tears streamed down onto my homework, blurring the ink. I didn't want to leave my school. I didn't want to leave my teachers, my friends. Mama — who was then still moving toward the future — took me into the bathroom and washed my flushed cheeks. She told me not to be afraid. I would have better teachers, friends who were better educated, a bigger school, with a playground. The house was in the Vedado, the very best section of Havana. At last we could leave this hellhole, central Havana. Mama — she who was heading into the future — was tearing my universe apart.

"But try to understand, child," she said. "And besides, the Dueñas, those girls you like so much? Yesterday I was talking to their mother, and they're leaving the country. So you're going to lose them anyway."

"You're lying, Mama! Why are you telling me all these lies? Why? They can leave, for all I care. I want to stay in my little house, in my little bed, with my little teddy bear and my fairy tales. Everyone's lying! Everyone's crazy!"

Everyone except Mama, that is. The Dueñas did run away to the United States. Mercedes with her long blond hair and green eyes. Lourdes with her long brown hair and green eyes. Chachita with her long red hair and green eyes. My childhood friends, engraved in my memory. Mama was telling the truth.

The Soviet car, the Lada, wasn't all that disastrous. I

barely noticed it. The real shock was when the president of the Committee for the Defense of the Revolution broke the seals and Papa opened the door of this enormous house in the Vedado. It was an architectural jewel, with a garden, an interior patio, another patio in the back. Papa walked in with a diffident air, suspicious of everything, checking out every corner, as if afraid of finding some vermin left over from the previous owner (I guessed this, because I heard him say that he didn't want to inherit anything from some *gusano*). Meanwhile, Mama was biting her nails in excitement. The president of the Committee for the Defense of the Revolution yawned and left. He still had a lot of work to do, lots of people to denounce, and he'd been up since before the crack of dawn to check out the comings and goings of the people on his block.

The house, which had belonged to a sculptor who fled to Florida, was filled with art. Mama took me by the hand and began to show me the objects. It was like we were in a museum. The humidity had wreaked havoc on the paintings — magnificent Cuban landscapes and classical portraits by Cuban artists now living in exile. Suddenly Mama stopped short in front of a painting.

"A Lam! An authentic Wifredo Lam!" she cried ecstatically.

"All that fuss over *that* doodle?" Papa asked.

Mama knew right then and there that she had made a terrible mistake falling in love with the son of a peasant — my paternal grandfather — who had loaned money to her father — my maternal grandfather — so that my mother and her brother could finish school in Havana. Mama had finished her studies before the Revolution, thanks to the money lent by her future father-in-law (as my father was forever reminding her), and after receiving her bachelor's degree, she went on to study art history. But when the triumph of the Revolution came, she abandoned her studies to join the tobacco harvest. Father, meanwhile, was taking a class at the University for Workers and Peasants. His father most definitely did not want him to become an engineer of any kind, for he believed, and believed with all his heart and soul, that the earth needed expert, loving hands and that working the earth was far more worthwhile than any university career. I had to help Papa with his math hundreds of times. He and I were at roughly the same level. Years later, it occurred to me that Mama had had to marry him to repay the money she had borrowed for her education. Still, though Papa may have been an uncouth peasant, he was an extremely handsome devil. He looked like the men in those paintings by Servando Cabrera. But however crazy about him she may have been in bed, they had almost nothing in common except their revolutionary work. He detested the theater, fell asleep the minute he went to the movies, and despised ballet. This was why he found it impossible to share Mama's admiration for antique furniture and china, all those bourgeois doodads and knick-knacks, not to mention the wasteful extravagance of the curtains with their purple flower pattern.

"I don't like this house," he declared dryly. With that he turned and headed toward the street.

Mama caught him just as he reached the door, planted herself in front of him, begged him, sobbed, got down on her knees and kissed his feet. He simply stood there, motionless. I couldn't bear the sight of such embarrassing melodrama and decided to snoop around the rest of the house. All the doors opened easily when I turned the knobs. The contents of the rooms both seduced and terrified me. There were whole rooms done in art nouveau style and paneled with precious wood; Tiffany lamps, Gallé vases, Lalique crystal, paintings, porcelain, English china, Persian rugs. Only one door, painted Pompeii green, resisted my efforts, but a sturdy kick with my orthopedic shoes (I was born with flat feet, and my arches needed support) did the trick. The room was suffused with a sepia light, like in one of those eerie Tarkovsky films. My eyes bulged, as I tried to take in what I found before me: naked men, motionless, standing on pedestals, watching me. Lots of naked men: some smiling, others more circumspect, still others frozen in a ferocious look or gesture, dancing some wild, ecstatic dance. One had a pink stomach, his fingers playing with his belly button. Gleaming black buttocks shone in the half-light of the room, and a solid, muscular hand firmly held a magnificent brown penis. I'd never seen anything like it. A massive, athletic chest, mulatto in color, with suspenders that barely grazed the dark nipples. I didn't know what to do in the presence of so much beauty. I was discovering male nudity, and I was delighted. A handsome young man, his forehead fringed with beguiling curls, was depicted slipping into sleep. His lips were so full, so sensual, so moist, so desirable . . . I dragged a little stool over to the statue, climbed up, and kissed his lips. He was cold, but I warmed him up with my flicking tongue. This was my first kiss, but I knew from a friend that when you kissed, you had to open your mouth and wiggle your tongue from right to left and up and down.

Enchanted by my discovery, I raced through the house, dancing as if I were in the corps of *Swan Lake*. Mama and Papa were standing by the main entrance, shaking their heads. Papa was still griping — my ears were three times sharper than they had ever been — about the house being haunted. And if proof were needed, here was his own daughter dancing like a whirling dervish through the corridors and rooms. Mama managed to grab me and shake me by the shoulders. I came to my senses.

"Mama, Papa! You won't believe it, but in one of the rooms there are statues of guys with their weenies and rumps showing!"

It was probably all my fault. Papa took off like a shot, heaving like a humped ox. He burst into the room, which immediately lost its mystical color. The sun spattered those glorious bodies with specks of light that were cruelly, unforgivably real. Then Papa ran off and found a stick and began hacking away at shoulder blades, breaking off feet and arms, cracking open cheeks and skulls, breaking torsos into pieces, pulverizing lips and penises, crushing to a pulp buttocks and armpits. The young men put up no resistance; their powdery and serene eyes disappeared, as if focused on some passionate eternity. I wanted to save them. When I came into the room, sunlight had blinded my eyes. When I could see again, it was all over. I began caressing the debris. Only then did I realize the full extent of my guilt. My father was gathering up the fragments and tossing them in the general direction of the door.

"Sculptor, my ass! Goddamn queer, that's what he is!"

Mama was pacing from one end of the room to the other, biting her fists to keep from crying out. When Papa had finished gathering all the bits and pieces into a big pile, he took a deep breath, filled his mouth with saliva, and spit furiously on the broken bodies of plaster and wood. The pieces of bronze and marble had also suffered mortal wounds, but the enormous provocative parts had somehow remained intact. Papa siphoned some gas from the tank of the Lada with the help of a little garden hose. He poured the liquid over the pile and lit a match. Within seconds a bonfire was raging. Always the same fire. The fire that every man carries deep within himself, the sole object of which is extermination.

"You should know that I intend to stay in this house," he said, breathing hard, "because I don't have the luxury to choose. But I want all these stinking ornaments and paintings out of here, and I mean now!"

Papa delivered this as a threat to my mother, who was completely done in by so much machismo and irreverence.

I gazed down at the mountain of martyred bodies. When you surrender your nubile lips to a statue, something strange and transcendent has to occur in your life. (Cubans are forever turning everything into a transcendental sign.) For a few brief moments I had fallen in love with a statue. And for a few brief moments too, I had turned myself into his denouncer, his torturer.

Filled with remorse, I clung tenaciously to the idea that I would not give up this house. Mama and I had our way. We moved into the new house immediately, she bringing her sad little gingham dresses and the Cuban flag that Che had draped over her pregnant belly. At first we occupied only a tiny portion of the house. We used one bedroom (I was afraid to sleep alone), the kitchen, which was so big we also used it as the dining room, and the bathroom, with its dark-blue tiles and granite floor. Little by little, we spread out and took possession of the other rooms, a process that paralleled my own growth. To everyone's surprise, as I grew up I integrated the furniture and all the ornaments into my daily life without the slightest problem, as if I had been to the manner born. Papa was a little jealous and was visibly uncomfortable about this, protesting that I seemed more the daughter of an exiled homosexual sculptor than his.

The years went by, and conditions in Cuba grew worse and worse. The country grew poorer and poorer.

The ultimatum my father had given my mother that first day — an ultimatum he had ended up forgetting about — namely, that we get rid of the works of art in the house, was fulfilled in spite of ourselves. My father was no longer even aware of the contents of the house. He came and went, totally caught up in his various revolutionary tasks, such as sugarcane harvest quotas and volunteer worker squads. The more food shortages there were, the more Mama was forced to sell off what she called "the treasures of the house." One day I came upon her in the living room, in a state of distress, clutching a Gallé vase. Facing her was a woman holding out a sack that contained a recently slaughtered pig. We would have enough pork for a month. She was forever bartering or selling something, at first to private parties, then to the shady Hernán Cortés shops run by the state. These shops exchanged mouthfuls of bread for valuable works of art. Mama sold our Bellini for fifty dollars, which she spent on toothpaste, soap, bouillon cubes, dubious-looking meat, and milk. The only Bellini in all of Cuba! It was a figure of Christ, and the appraiser looked at it, shook it as if it were a dry gourd to make sure there were no gold coins hidden inside, then said distractedly:

"Pancho, note this down: 'One more holy work, a crucifixion, large, weighs a lot.' Give her . . . let me see let me see . . . fifty dollars. Be on your way now, woman. You did well."

Mama was inconsolable. She knew how much the

Bellini was really worth. Unpayable, like our foreign debt. She was determined to try and keep one work of art: the doodle she held so near and dear, the Wifredo Lam.

But when in 1967 they assassinated Che, my mother began to "take leave of herself," as they say. He was her idol. She adored him far more than the other heroes of the Revolution, like Jorge Negrete and Pedro Infante. I remember coming home from school one day and finding her with the Cuban flag draped around her head, wailing and moaning so loud it broke my heart.

"But why? But why? But why?" she kept bellowing over and over again. Papa just looked at her, silent as a tomb, his eyes filled with tears, a stunned expression on his face. I went over to her and planted a kiss on the flag's star, which was right over her forehead. Mama never recovered from Che's death. Over and over again she read the *Diario de Bolivia*, caressing the printed characters as if they were Che's own bloodstained hair, as if she were present at the murder scene, gazing on the shining, half-closed eyes of the Heroic Warrior.

As for my father, he went on working like a maniac and was appointed as a high official in the workers' union — secretary-general of the Party. He belonged to every organization, both human and divine. He was in the Territorial Militia. He was in the forefront of the Committee for the Defense of the Revolution. And he was in line to become a candidate to the Delegado del Poder Popular — the People's Power Organization. Family life became more and more complicated. Father was almost never home; rarely did he show up for dinner. We began to see him more and more onstage at political rallies and on the evening news. He'd been bitten by the bug that begets speeches. By the time I got my first period, I had suffered enough from the lack of a father, and since Mama was off meeting other wives in the Women's Federation, to exchange the latest gossip and watch the latest soap opera — which comes to the same thing — I began to sneak out at night, into the street and into bad habits. Which is how I met the Traitor.

My mother — now Madame Elsewhere — suffered a number of near-fatal blows. My father was one of those who predicted publicly that the goal of ten million tons of sugarcane would not be met, for which he received an official reprimand. He took the reprimand badly and began wandering aimlessly through the streets of Havana, in a state of dementia. Without even realizing where he was, he went one day to the gates of the Mazorra insane asylum, grabbed hold of the bars of the fence that surrounded it.

"Let me out of here!" he began to shout at the top of his lungs.

Everyone — passersby, patients, visitors, people both inside and outside the psychiatric hospital — took him literally. He was confusing the inside and outside of the hospital. He wasn't completely wrong. For him, the crazies were the ones on the outside, and the normal people were inside; and in his hysterical state he saw the streets as cells.

Anyway, they locked him up for six months. When he came out he was stammering and stuttering, no doubt the result of the electroshocks. Mama was waiting for him, but she was already half gone herself and only vaguely aware of her husband's ordeal. Names and dates escaped her, virtually every remark made her laugh, and she slept all the time.

Just as Father had predicted, the sugarcane goal of Ten Million Tons was in fact not achieved, and he was rewarded with some insignificant decoration for his foresight. Elsa, meanwhile, was moving steadily toward Elsewhere.

Another near-fatal blow for Mama was my divorce from the Traitor and my refusal to move back to our house. She asked me, her hands folded in supplication, to please come back. Your parents are still your parents, she said, and a family is important. A divorced woman is not only open to slander but a target for men with evil intentions. You'll see, I'll take good care of you, like a baby. But I didn't go back. It pained me to see her growing old.

I moved in with a friend, the Gusana. That was the third blow to Elsewhere's psyche. The Gusana was fed up with politics, and long before occasional prostitution was popular, she threw herself into it with passion. In her heart — and in her gut — she was a pioneer. One day she got her papers in order and married a fat Spaniard much older than she, then left the country, bequeathing me her apartment. From then on, my progenitors lost any remaining right to control my private life. They ceased to be my parents and became my children.

Now that he's retired, my father spends his days making wood carvings — little men, all exactly alike, each one tall and proud, brandishing a machete in his right hand. Later, he sells them in the park between Linea and L streets. Elsewhere looks at me disconsolately. I ask her where she put the latest Brazilian potboiler, and she answers:

"Do you remember olives?"

"Mama, did you see the film last Saturday?"

"Do you remember ground steak, real ground steak, the kind that comes from cows? Not that lousy stuff they make out of soya. I mean red meat, the kind you have to chew and chew."

"Mama, do you have any news from Uncle?"

"And that cider we used to have at Christmas? Did you ever get a chance to taste it?"

"Mama, why haven't you taken your pill?"

"And the little tamales they made out of corn and pork?"

She swallows her saliva. I'm still holding a glass of water in my hand and the meprobamate — exchanged for some Benadryl from a neighbor with allergies — in the other. Elsewhere's chin begins to tremble. She murmurs to me to close the window. It's cold outside. It's ninety-six in the shade.

"Child, do you think he's coming back to take our house away?"

"Who, Mama?"

I pick her up and carry her over to the bed. She weighs nothing, a sack of feathers. I tuck her in.

"Who do you think? The sculptor! If he comes back from Miami, he'll toss us into the street. He'll make a fire out of us, the way your father did with his sculptures!"

"No, Mama, the sculptor won't do that. Anyway, maybe he's dead."

"No, my child. What are you talking about? Of course he's not dead."

"What makes you so sure, Mama?"

"Because I haven't been able to give him back his Wifredo Lam. And no one who owns a painting as beautiful as that can ever die without seeing it again."

And with that she falls asleep, rigid, her eyelids fluttering in the general direction of Elegguá, god of paths and ways, whose small statue bewitches the bedroom and bathes it with light.

6

The Gusana

Only glass breaks, men die on their feet.

— Popular Cuban slogan

THOUGH IT'S NOT TIME YET, the workday is over. The power went off again, and the copying machine, the computer, and the typewriters are all electric. The new girl who's working on the database lost everything because she didn't save in time. Tomorrow she'll have to start all over and input the same information, and probably the power will go off again just as she's on the verge of reconstituting the database, and so she'll have to start all over the next day from scratch. And so on and so forth, time without end, amen.

It has rained, and the parking area doesn't have a roof, so my bicycle is soaked. The pavement is muddy. My clothes are going to be a total mess by the time I get home. I'll have to carry up some water to wash them, to wash myself, and to make dinner. With any luck, the power will not have been cut off at my house — which is in another part of the Vedado — in which case, the motors will have kicked in and filled my secret reservoirs with water, and I won't have to carry it up eight flights. (I had to install the tanks very early in the morning, because the law allows only one tank per apartment and I now have three, hidden in the air vents.)

As soon as I put my feet on the pedals of my Chinese bike, I begin thinking of you, my darling little Gusana. I met you at the teachers' college, during one of those trips I made to bribe the dean. You were studying geography, and we hit it off right away, became friends despite the Traitor's distrust. He couldn't stand the thought of you. I would sneak out of the apartment to go and meet you, and on borrowed bicycles we would ride off together to the Malecón, gabbing and making fun of the world. In those days, riding a bicycle meant you were either a floozy or an out-and-out prostitute, so people used to shout insults at us. We couldn't have cared less. We laughed so loudly and insolently that not only did we spook those who yelled at us, but we made the cops' hair stand on end. One guard of the CD, the Committee for the Defense of the Revolution, reported us to his superiors, maintaining that at least two nights a week we went — *by bicycle!* — to the Hotel Deauville, where we sat for hours and hours, on the jetty overlooking the sea, smoking Populares, Cuban filter tips. The guard strongly suspected that we were using the glow of our cigarettes to send signals to the Yankee imperialists.

In the bicycle department, we were pioneers.

If you were to come back today, you'd be completely shocked. Havana is sad, dilapidated, broken down. Look at that man over there, at the corner of G and Seventeenth, the one poking around in the garbage cans with a spoon. He carefully cleans the greasy plastic wrapping and then gulps down the rotting remains of whatever he finds. He couldn't be more than thirty. I don't want to stop. I pedal faster and faster, recklessly risking life and limb as I cross the avenue. I don't want see the truth. My generation was not prepared for it. I know there's wretchedness throughout Latin America, but other countries didn't experience revolution, didn't have to listen to the bullshit about "building a better world." I can't see this better world.

Do you remember the long lines we stood in to buy those Italian ices that were all the rage then?

Do you remember the ice cream and cake they served at the parlor on the corner of Prado Avenue and Neptune Street?

Do you remember the Rialto movie house, where they used to show art films?

Do you remember the croquettes they called Soyuz 15, which stuck to the roof of your mouth?

Do you remember the cafeteria in the Manzana de Gómez shopping center?

Do you remember spaghetti?

Do you remember that awful drink made somewhere in the Eastern bloc that was supposed to be just as good as Coca-Cola?

Do you remember the bread sprinkled with sugar? The rum cocktail made with lime juice and crushed basil, virtually guaranteed to give you violent diarrhea? The pieces of bread with guava marmalade made by God-knows-who at that little shop in Obispo Street?

Do you remember the Palace of the Flies, the Europa Pizzeria?

Do you remember the bazaar where the old men used to hang out? Today, in that same neighborhood, authorized vendors sell imitation art deco rocking chairs, Creole style. The old men are slowly starving to death.

Do you remember the cookies in the Lluvia de Oro bar?

Do you remember the beans at the Castillo Farnés?

Do you remember the Bodeguita del Medio when it was still bohemian?

Do you remember the Caballero from Paris, the Chinese comic and her jokes, the incoherent speeches Charlie used to spout, the Marquesa, with her tight curls dyed bright purple?

Do you remember the extra buses they put into service to take us to the eastern beaches?

Do you remember the beaches, the buses? Does all that ring any bells?

Do you remember the hibiscus, the flowers they used to call *mar pacífico*, or the butterflies of the Vedado?

Do you remember the trees on Prado Avenue, near the statue of Zenea?

Do you remember the bookstores?

Do you remember the traffic on Neptune Street?

Do you remember San Rafael Boulevard, with its pizza parlors? And the movie theaters, the Rex and the Duplex, both closed now for repairs?

Do you remember the things they used to sell on the open market? Milk for one peso, yogurt by the liter. Do you remember cream cheese and butter?

Do you remember the Wakamba, the Karabalí? Going to those places is like going to Mars. They're not so much cafeterias as offshoots of foreign companies. Everything has to be paid for in dollars. Cuban currency? Use it to wipe yourself! Do you remember local currency?

Do you remember the synthetic ham — three pesos a pound?

Do you remember the nightclubs where you got felt up? Do you remember the tryst houses?

Do you remember air-conditioning? Do you remember the overhead fans?

Do you remember the light?

༺༻

We survived, with stomachs bloated or closed for repairs. Nothing existed. Only the Party is immortal.

I'm stuck with my bicycle on the narrow second-floor landing of my building. Hernia, who had taken up arms against the sea and all sorts of other troubles, appeared, brandishing an airmail letter. Without a word or gesture, she hoisted my bike and helped me carry it up to the third floor.

"You got a letter from Spain!" she said with a complicitous wink. She vanished into her maritime grotto as quickly as she had appeared.

It has to be from you. Of course it's from you. My darling Gusana, all I had to do was think about you and you appeared, my faithful phantom, my soul mate. I was waiting for news from you with Gothic anxiety. Tell me everything, no matter how banal. You have no idea of the incredible dreams I have had, thanks to your letters. I see myself in the Prado Museum, standing in front of some Goya or El Greco, or before that extraordinary painting by Patinir, *Charon Crossing the River Styx*. I see myself gazing at Bosch's *Garden of Earthly Delights* and being depressed by it; or studying the faces in Velázquez's *Meninas*. I picture you doing your shopping in the Corte Inglés, going to the cinema or the theater on the Grand Vía, wondering which volume of poems to buy in the Visor bookstore. How does gazpacho taste? I saw it being made in Almodóvar's film *Women on the Verge of a Nervous Breakdown*.

I turn my key in the door. I gaze expectantly at the light switch. Now is the moment of the great anxiety, the moment of truth. My happiness depends on what happens when I push the switch. I push. Let there be light. And there is!

I lay my bicycle next to the sofa. Its wheels have made a muddy mess of the floor. I go into the bathroom. Before I read your letter I have to clean up. I brush my teeth, wash my face, comb my hair, change into some clean, comfortable clothes. I stretch out on the sofa and tear open the airmail envelope.

Madrid, Dawn

Dearest Yocandra,

I received your letter but I have to tell you that when I read it I couldn't believe it was from you. All you talk about is your Chinese bicycle, the power outages, the sugared water you drink to ease your hunger, and a fabulous Nihilist, who is the only thing I envy you for. Your letters are straight out of the nineteenth century.

The latest news from a Cuban martyr. You keep saying that I shouldn't worry about it, you don't need a thing. But as far as I can see, except for sex, you lack everything. As for me, it's the complete opposite: my principal needs are more or less satisfied, but in the sex department it's a complete disaster.

As I've already told you in other letters, my FOM (Fat Old Man), my bald-as-a-coot, red-as-a-beet moaner-and-groaner, is so awful that even our blessed Mary Magdalene on the brink of starvation would turn him down. It also appears that he doesn't have nearly as much money as he led me to believe in Havana. In Cuba, anyone who takes you out for dinner, even at a third-class hotel, can pass for a millionaire. In short, my love, I've had it up the wazoo with this old fart, who seems unable or unwilling to keep from unleashing the loudest, most embarrassing belches — both at home or, more likely, in public places. If only they hadn't instituted that damn ration book, which I couldn't stand any longer. If only there hadn't been all those endless speeches, all that demagoguery. If only the head of the CDR hadn't threatened to turn in his own son if he didn't do his stint at guard duty. If only those women of the Federation hadn't spent all their time making revolutionary dolls out of rags. If only the Pioneers — poor little souls, so young and already mired in mediocrity — hadn't recited those poems extolling the triumph of the Revolution. All those children in their berets and neck-

erchiefs marching down the avenues, shouting: "Give
me an F! ... Give me an I! ... Give me a D! ..."
etc., etc. Blah blah blah. Just thinking about it convinces
me that if I had to do it all over again, I'd still have
married my FOM without a second's hesitation, even if
he swore he was from Burkina Faso. And you know
better than anyone that I could never, I mean *never*,
stand fat men.

Why don't you find yourself a lover, you'll say.
There you go again with your nineteenth-century men-
tality! Here lovers cost a fortune, and the best you can
hope for is that when you go out he'll split the tab with
you. The fact is there are plenty of good-looking men
with dark, limpid eyes, rosy cheeks, jet-black hair, and
blood-red lips (from all the fruit they eat, probably).
Real Snow Whites just waiting to be poisoned by an
apple. But, Light of My Life, guess what? Most of these
guys are homosexuals and want nothing to do with
women. If they were only a little faggy I wouldn't care.
I'm not prejudiced, you know. But they're allergic to
pussy. All they're interested in is dick. A grievous lack on
our part. I walk around the streets of Madrid with a
package of condoms in my pocketbook, but they'll end
up rotting from lack of use. I bought them the minute
we landed at the airport. I might as well have thrown the
money out the window. You won't believe me, and I'm
sure this will shock you to death, but I have even con-
templated becoming a lesbian. Here you see all sorts of

films featuring women with enormous tits, erect nipples, firm asses, and they're all fondling one another. First thing you know, you feel your panties getting all moist, and then almost despite yourself you end up having an orgasm as you watch two women sucking away at each other. Guess what? That's the kind of video my Great White Whale likes to rent. Anyway, according to several magazines here, sex between women is more dangerous because of AIDS. With men, you slip on a rubber and that's that. But they haven't yet invented a safe-sex face mask — that's my term for it anyway — for pussies. And when the innocent-looking watery cream begins to flow, who's to say millions of deadly bacteria aren't just waiting to invade you, like in all those horror movies?

Once, I went to the sauna, where you go not to lose weight but to hook up with someone. All I could come up with was an old dame with peroxide-blond hair, dark roots and all, a veritable monument to plastic surgery: face, breasts, buttocks, hips, and God knows what else. I didn't stick around. One look, and I was out the door! I swear that after that experience, if I met Claudia Schiffer and Linda Evangelista I would throw up all over them.

The museums? Yes, I've gone a number of times. The Prado is very poorly lit, and the paintings are packed in every which way. The postcards and posters all cost money. I bought a little notebook, with the idea of describing the paintings — you know, their main char-acteristics and who painted them — so I wouldn't forget them and could describe them to you in my letters. You know how absentminded I am: I left the notebook somewhere. It'll turn up one of these days. You have no idea how upset I was about losing it. I spent the entire day in the damn museum, until the guard came and threw me out. Another time I went to the Military Museum in Retiro Park. I went up to the top floor, and just as you had asked me to, I found Antonio Maceo's saddle. I caressed it for you. My sweet, only you could get so emotional about such nonsense. His saddle is no different from any other, assuming that the saddle really *is* his. These Spaniards have complexes that haven't even been invented yet. They're the only people I know who can fart higher than their asshole: they haven't the slightest compunction about reinventing Egypt, maintaining, with dictionaries of the period to prove it and with the Virgin Mary as their witness, that Nefertiti was originally from Madrid.

I know this will upset you, but I have to say it anyway, so you don't have any great illusions about the Spaniards. Below the general's saddle is a little card that reads:

SADDLE ONCE BELONGING TO THE CUBAN GENERAL
ANTONIO MACEO. SPANISH WAR TROPHY.

That "War Trophy" hit me like a ton of bricks.

Anyway, I left the country to try and get away from

all the political crap, and here I am, politically aware up
to my eyeballs. El Fatso buys me every newspaper under
the sun, so that I'll be able to converse with his jerk-off
buddies and their wives. Every last one of them — the
wives, I mean — are old witches, and three times a
week, at least, they are the recipients of a world-class
thrashing, which is the reason they all wear scarves and
sunglasses. They've formed a club — The Satisfied
Wives Club. Can't you just picture it? And when they
want to slip out to meetings, they have to dream up
some story for the husbands: "Honey? I'm just going out
to buy a little ham for dinner, okay?" I'm no dummy. I
got myself named treasurer. That way I can put enough
aside so that one day in the not too distant future I can
found my own club. I'll call it the Expatriate Cuban
Hustlers Club. Here in Madrid, all kinds of Cuban girls
come to see me when they can, mostly pretty little half-
breeds still in their teens and black girls with spiked hair,
abandoned by the guys who brought them out of
Cuba — unless *they* dumped the men. A lot of them
become prostitutes, but they have to do it quietly, since
their papers usually aren't legal. Most of the time they're
scared to death of being caught, and they're hungry and
cold. Being a prostitute in the summer is one thing.
Winter is a whole different matter.

I told you I read all the daily papers, including the
international edition of *Le Monde*, which is very intel-
lectual. It's pretty boring, but it's the only paper that
really tells you what's happening in Cuba. And in case
you're not aware, no one on the face of this earth — not
even God Himself — gives a good goddamn what's
going on there. In fact, I'm sure He's regretting He ever

created the place. People here are obsessed with money, with wars, and with the immigrants from the Eastern bloc who are arriving in droves and taking jobs away from half the human race, for the simple reason that they're cheap. You can find a Russian scientist who'll work in a lab, doing all kinds of complicated experiments for a couple of dollars. At night that same guy will be driving a taxi. Which reminds me, my sweet. The Russians here smell just as bad as they did in Cuba. So you see it can't be the lack of deodorant. It's part of their nature. They're just a sour bunch. Whenever I see one coming, I run as fast as I can in the opposite direction and open the volume of Pushkin you gave me. As far as I'm concerned, he's the only Russian who gives them a good name.

On the subject of newspapers and literature, if ever you decide one day to write a best-seller, in *El País,* on the same page where they have the weather and the obituaries, there are announcements about literary contests, which not only promise big prize money but also guarantee to publish your book. If you ever decide to write one, remember I'm here.

You're probably wondering how I can read the international edition of *Le Monde.* The reason is, this summer I took a French course, because Moby Dick is saving up to take me to Paris. Can you picture me in the City of Light? I'll send you pictures with the Eiffel Tower in the background.

Yes, it's true. Every day I buy a shitload of knick-knacks. Here buying is a vice, and when it comes to that, I'm utterly depraved. It's in my blood. And television corrupts. On that point I'll say the Cubans are absolutely right on the mark: advertising really is the enemy, especially of your pocketbook. You would not believe it. They get you coming and going. Today it's a bottle of shampoo you simply have to have. Tomorrow it's the rinse. The next day it's a depilatory, or ice cream, or candy, or one kind of soap and then another (one made from goat's milk and glycerin — the morning perfume, don't you know, which means you need another for the afternoon and still another for evening). Don Rafael del Junco — remember him? the guy in the story our mothers used to tell us? — well, here he's on television. You can even catch him on the radio. In fact, I even saw him once in a movie. Anyway, every day I go to the Corty — that's the new name for the Corte Inglés — and spend a fortune on hairpins, different kinds of toothbrushes, little dresses on sale because they have some tiny defect, cheap perfume. And I stuff my face — I can't get enough chorizos and those Jijona nougats.

Here you have to eat a lot, and because dieting and cold weather don't go together, I've put on weight. I'm a hundred and ten now, twenty pounds more than when I arrived. I've changed — I'm older and more realistic, and the cold has cured my asthma. But not my nuttiness — I'm as crazy as ever. I'm not homesick for Cuba. All I really miss are you and the sea. Marrying the Old Poop meant I had to give up my Cuban citizenship. It also meant tons of paperwork, but nothing to slit your wrists over. In my heart I'm still more Cuban than the palm trees, and no one can ever change that. Yet I'm not some raving nationalist, by any means. I keep reminding myself that José Martí spent most of his life abroad, and he's still as Cuban as they come.

Anyway, there was no way I could have stayed there any longer. Whenever I remember that political slogan telling us we had to die on our feet, my feet ache. Whoever could have dreamed up such a stupid slogan anyway? If I remember right, only glass breaks, "men die on their feet!" I'm not made of glass, but I have the gall to hope that I'll die like most of the human race. Once, someone tried to put me down by claiming that that dumb-ass slogan came from Martí himself. If it's true, even Martí could put his foot in his mouth once in a while. No one's perfect twenty-four hours a day.

And these guys bound for extinction cling to those shreds, those slogans, still believing their path is the one and only, the true way, the irreproachable, the indispensable, the inevitable. They can't bring themselves to see they're unbearable and that the reality they've imposed is unlivable. Fuck 'em! Life is more than boot camp.

Yoqui, what more can I say? Madrid is kind of filthy and swarming with tourists. The people who live here aspire to nothing more than trying to act like Americans. There's an exciting nightlife, but I'm not part of it. First off because I can't leave my Behemoth by himself, but also because I don't dare go out alone at night. Besides, what would be the point of parading my loneliness on sidewalks that will never belong to me? Sometimes for days on end all I do is exchange a few brief words with Sleepyhead. He's busy trying to drive me crazy. It's his way of getting back at me for my obvious revulsion — no matter how hard I try, I can't hide it — every time he gets undressed in front of me. Is this what I have to look forward till my dying day? I hope not! Someday I'll kill him, or find a way to buy my freedom. Although getting a divorce is a real nightmare. My goal is to earn some money and get the hell out of here. How, exactly, I'm going to pull that off I haven't figured out. So you see? It's like a Hollywood film!

In closing, I'm going to bring up my major reason for writing, which I wanted to ask you about. I'm sure you're aware that the Lynx left Cuba just a month ago on a homemade raft. The raft was shipwrecked, and everybody in it was drowned except him. He was picked up by an American ship that found the remains of the raft drifting with the currents, his body strapped to a beam by a piece of rope. To make a long story short, he survived and has recovered — at least that's what I was told. He called me the other day. Big surprise! I couldn't help scolding him. What for Christ's sake did he think he was doing? He could easily have drowned. He seemed a little confused and very sad, which I found strange, given his usual optimism. But he was full of plans for the future, as only someone who has felt the wings of death brush him can be.

Let's pray for him. You'll be hearing from me again, sooner than you think. If I can convince my Polar Bear to let me, I'll call you. If I don't call you more often, it's because it's so incredibly expensive.

A metallic kiss to your bike. May there be much light in your life, and may the Nihilist be with you forever. Don't introduce him to me, because I'll steal him. When you gaze out at the sea, pray to Yemayá for me and the Lynx. Don't forget us. An endless kiss.

Your Gusana

I had cried so much in my life — wailing like some wild beast — that my tear ducts were completely dry, but, my Gusana, your letter brought up sobs from the depths of my soul. The circle is finally closed. We're condemned to be dispersed throughout the world, exposed to danger, prey to the most acute pain in the fathomless pit of our consciousness, forced to renounce our dreams, our very selves. I remember your love for the Lynx. He was the kind of man who drove you crazy, who could infuriate you like no one else, yet you adored him. He was the love of your life. But you couldn't face an uncertain future as a *micro-brigadista*, filled with children — for though he had a degree in art history, he worked as a mason and slept on an inflatable mattress under stairwells. You weren't ready to take care of him, even if he was the man of your life, because you could never suffer fools who could talk only about the Greeks and the Egyptians and nothing else. You were forced to choose between marrying the Lynx, then spending your life in some miserable government housing project in Alamar, and taking up with your Spanish Dinosaur, who invited you to hotels with swimming pools, bought you expensive dresses, and dined you in dollar-economy restaurants. You chose the latter. And your present life, my darling Gusana, strikes me like a cabaret without the rumba. Calvary itself. As for the Lynx, a few months after you'd left, he got his apartment. Two months after that, he was able to exchange it for a house in Miramar, a superb spread, though it had no electricity, no bottled gas, no water (the pump that supplied the precious liquid to that part of town wasn't working). But you know the Lynx always lands on his feet. He's one of the luckiest creatures alive. He rediscovered his passion for painting and sent off one of his works to an international competition in Japan. Guess what? He won first prize, which brought him thousands of dollars. (They no longer put people in prison for possession of foreign currency.) He used the money to outfit his mansion. He bought a generator; he bought bottled gas from a legal company that dealt only with private parties paying in dollars; he put in a cistern, fixed the motor, installed reservoirs made out of ferro-cement that could store water; he painted the house and hung his paintings. He also bought and refinished gorgeous antique furniture, furnishing himself an English dining room, a Louis XV living room, and an art deco bedroom. It was all miraculous. The old-timers who lived in the Vedado sold all that kind of thing for a pittance.

Flashback. Preface to the next chapter:

They waited until the Lynx had finished his work. He was sitting in his French-style armchair when the doorbell rang. He opened the door.

"We're members of the Committee for the Defense of the Revolution. We're here on the authority of the President himself to denounce you as a profiteer and have come to confiscate 'your' property. You're to accompany the lieutenant, here."

The Lynx responded with a dazzling smile. "Wait here just a minute," he said, and ran off to get his certificate proving that he had indeed won the Japanese prize and the receipt from the bank proving that he had legally deposited the prize money. He produced them. But of course none of these cretins understood Japanese. They loaded everything, including the Lynx's own paintings, onto a truck, and locked and sealed the house. The Lynx was tried and found guilty. He was about to be sent away to the Combinado Prison when (I'm telling you, the man was born lucky and is protected by Our Lady of Grace, adored Obbatalá!) some high-ranking Japanese minister appeared out of nowhere. It turned out that he was the one who had bought the Lynx's prize-winning painting and wanted to learn more about this esteemed artist. The police nearly went out of their minds trying to find him. The state's entire security apparatus went into action. Where in hell did we put this damn-fool genius? The Lynx, meanwhile, was pacing the floor of his cell when they found him. Get him out of there! Now! The Lynx hasn't the faintest idea why they are hauling him out of his cell and hustling him along, with kicks in the ass, back through the prison corridors. They bathe him, clothe him, and take him over to a suite in the Hotel Nacional.

He had a three-minute interview with the Japanese minister, who smiled and bowed and scraped the whole time.

All the Lynx said was hello when the man arrived and good-bye when he left. The Japanese minister gave him a bonsai planted especially for his favorite painter, before an aide came into the room, whispered something in his ear, and escorted the minister off to some meeting.

When the Lynx returned to his suite, the chambermaid was already changing the sheets. She had been informed by the management that the gentleman's reservation had expired.

The Lynx found himself in the middle of the Rampa — that fabulous asphalt valley that from far away looks as if the sea is suspended in the air — holding a very special bonsai in his right hand but without his inflatable mattress (confiscated with his other things) and without a stairwell under which to spend the night.

End of flashback.

We are born guilty, and each of our acts loosens the rope holding aloft the guillotine's blade. It falls, and our heads drop onto the straw of history.

I hope to see you again, my beloved chrysalis, and you will be transformed into a fluttering, spinning butterfly. And perhaps I will sprout new petals, like a rose that has never been plucked.

7

The Lynx

> I see Rome pass before my eyes,
> my house and everything therein,
> and for each place, scenes of which
> they were the theater spring to life.
>
> —Ovid, *Tristia*

Y THOUGHTS FILLED WITH the alienation born of solitude. This alienation is not mine alone. I know how alone the Lynx must feel. Does he know how I feel? Even when I'm with other people? What brought us together, what forged our indestructible friendship, was the daily pain, the terror of suddenly realizing how useless we were, our hatred for the *nada*, the nothingness. We were young. We wanted to work, to give our all in this life, the only one we had. We despised the endless stasis of our lives, this paralyzing anguish in which we were drowning. We lived in exile from ourselves, our souls banished, our bodies responding obediently to the demands of the circumstances. Because to each person, each thing, we had to provide a response. Precooked meat. To doubt was out of the question, the mark of a nonbeliever. He was tired of being obedient. (We were the monks of blind obedience, and as was the case during the Inquisition, we crumbled before the calcinated corpses. An implacable, bloody burden bends our spines. The lucky generation, the ones who taste the fruits of victory, bear the painful weight of too much glory. We can never stand up proud and tall, because of the guilt we feel about those who faced the firing squads. Even if we ground our teeth, we went on believing the editorials in *Granma*. And sometimes our reasons for believing were obscure.)

When I met him, all I could think of was how he could have played Marcel Proust in a film. It was uncanny. The same nose, with its thin, straight bridge; a certain Arab look, which he owed to his genes; intense, dreamy, dark-brown eyes; long eyelashes; thick eyebrows; romantic dark circles under the eyes. Black hair, soft yet unruly, straight at the root but curly around his neck, meaning that no matter how he combed it, it always flopped over his forehead, forming a natural part in the middle. A mouth that always had a ready response; fine, even teeth and jutting chin; ears that stuck out just a bit. He was proud of his mustache, but I talked him into shaving it off. If this meant he lost a touch of his Proustian mystery, he acquired a certain resemblance to Al Pacino.

We became friends much later on, but I knew the second I met him that he was unusual. The night we saw a video of *Taxi Driver* at the house of some mutual friends sealed our bond. While VCRs were fairly common everywhere else in the world, they had just made their appearance in Havana, the City of Technology. As always, we were the last people on the planet to get the word, and as always, we blamed it all on the American embargo. He was the only one who knew how to push the buttons of this machine. If one of the guests had to go to the bathroom, he stopped the tape. We thought this was magical. And not only could he stop the video, he could make it go fast forward, or rewind it, using a little machine that he called his "control," teaching others how to use it, so that we wouldn't feel like such idiots. The film was in English, so he interpreted it for us. He was fluent in several languages. When the video was over, we had a few drinks, then left. I saw him discreetly remove his inflatable mattress — which was flat and neatly folded — from under his chair. Saying good night to me, he simply shook my hand, but he escorted the Gusana back to her house and left her at the door, a true gentleman. Then he took a short stroll through the neighborhood to give her a chance to turn in. When her lights went out, he came back. Before going into her building, he took a deep breath of fresh air, holding it jealously in his lungs. As soon as he was safely inside, he used that sweet night air to inflate his mattress. Little did the Gusana know that when she came down the stairs the next morning she was stepping over the body of her beloved.

The Lynx had got into trouble at college more than once. For one thing, he always wore a beret and the kind of tight pants the Beatles used to wear. He wasn't worried about looking different. He knew that in the art history department, tolerance had always prevailed. But one day the professor of ethics, a socialist realist virago, came into the classroom, strode straight over to him, grabbed the beret, and ripped it off his head.

"Aha! Now we see what this student was hiding under his beret: long hair!"

Long hair, it turned out, was her obsession, her pet peeve, and as far as she was concerned, it looked good only on women. She took out a pair of scissors and cut it off.

He struck back by remarking that Che Guevara had had long hair and wore a beret. That really set her off. She began screaming at him. The only thing he had in common with Che was that he suffered from asthma.

The Lynx charged again: "As long as I can remember, people have told us to be like Che. Well, that's what I've done."

Furious, the socialist realist virago pulled a knife from the folds of her gray skirt and pushed its shiny blade against the Lynx's windpipe.

"To be like Che, you have to have balls. You miserable excuse for a faggot, you've never had any in your whole stinking, goddamn life!"

Tears filled the Lynx's eyes. He had never been so humiliated, so powerless. Not only was a woman screaming at him, she was an elderly woman. He swallowed, and the point of the dagger pierced his skin. Drops of blood spilled down onto his white nylon shirt. She got down on her knees. For a second, he thought she was going to ask for his forgiveness, say that it was all a big joke, or who knows, maybe she was even going to give him a blow job. At the thought of that possibility, the faintest trace of a smile appeared on his face. Then his lips spread into a grimace of stupid ecstasy. But a rip and a tug down by his feet brought him back to reality. The socialist realist virago had cut off his Beatles pants — his only pair of tight-fitting jeans — for which he had traded his five-month quota of rice! The virago, still squatting, looked up at him triumphantly from her position on the floor, a string of gray mucus hanging from her nose.

He was not expelled. That would have been absurd. He had just defended his thesis with highest honors and was waiting for the school to send him his diploma. But it had been a close call. From then on, he knew that he would have to get away.

By chance, he was sent off to Moa to do his social service. He was put in charge of the local Institute of

Culture — which didn't exist. He was to build it from the ground up. They gave him the most miserable plot of land on the face of the planet, plus a shovel, a pickax, a hammer, and all the materials necessary to construct a modest cement building. The Lynx didn't get his name for nothing. What did he do? The minute he hit town, and without even dusting off his clothes from the long voyage, he strode into the village square, like Martí before the statue of Bolivár, and got everyone out of bed by reciting through a megaphone a poem by the Greek poet Constantine Cavafy. The villagers peered out of their doors, half asleep and amazed, yawning loudly, coughing, clearing their throats, the women rubbing their rheumy eyes without the slightest touch of coquettishness. They formed a widening circle around the Lynx. Gradually they seemed less daunted. A timid smile even began to appear here and there. They were beginning to understand the poem, especially the last part:

Why, so suddenly, this concern and confusion?
(How serious the faces have become once again!)
Why are the streets and the squares so empty,
And all the people gone home so gloomily?

Because night has fallen and the barbarians haven't come.
Some have come back from the frontiers,
Saying there are no barbarians.

And what will become of us without barbarians?
These people, when all is said and done, are our salvation.

When he finished, there was a burst of applause and
cheers. The following day, the inhabitants of Moa began
helping the Lynx to build their Institute of Culture. The
Lynx laid the first stone. When the building was finished
(in record time), he brought in famous poets, renowned
painters, popular jazz groups, and leading composers and
musicians; he put on plays and screened films that had
been banned for reasons no one could remember. News of
the cultural miracle began to spread. By now the Lynx was
in a complete trance, a trance of artistic and political
identity. An erotic feeling of heroic immortality suffused
him. So he was summoned back to Havana, the Experi-
mental City, presumably to replicate the exploit. All further aid to Moa was cut off, and the village fell back into
obscurity.

Things didn't go as well on the outskirts of Havana.
They gave him a ramshackle shanty in the remote village
of Mamoncillo, two miles from the nearest house. When
he asked how he was supposed to get cement, sand, the
flagstones for the floor, the slabs for the siding, and the
tools with which to construct the building, no one could
tell him. He ran around for an entire month — from the
Department of Building Permits to the warehouses where

the various materials were stored, and back again. He still managed to build a traditional campesino house made of palm fronds and, what was more, succeeded in filming an episode of the series *Palm Trees and Sugarcane,* in collaboration with Cuban Television. One day he gave up. (Giving up is our most serious weakness.) He asked to be transferred as a graphic artist to a literary review, the same literary review where I work today, thanks to him. Before that I was a "Cultural Documenter," an impressive-sounding title that in reality was total bullshit, a sinecure that involved cutting out all the articles in the foreign press that mentioned our country, or sending stupid letters and acknowledgments to "friends of our country." In most cases these were the most mediocre members of all the leftist regimes around the world, those to whom no one in their own countries paid any attention, but who came to visit Cuba, got themselves put up in the best five-star hotels, were given all they could eat and drink — without having to pay a peso — and promised Cuba all sorts of aid, which never seemed to materialize.

Then one day the editor in chief of the literary magazine went on a trip abroad and never came back. We were about to put the next issue of the magazine to bed, and we couldn't find any "able-bodied" — read "militant" — staffers because they were all off "volunteering" in the fields, or more to the point, raping the earth, for one has to love working the land to do it right. We had a crisis meeting. The Lynx raised his hand. He had made up his mind. In situations like that, you have to act fast. He asked for the floor and, with a great deal of self-assurance, nominated me as editor in chief. At that point he was still in good standing, and his suggestion was accepted without the slightest hesitation. In fact, it wasn't even submitted to the higher authorities for approval. From then on we became pals, brother and sister. For reasons that remain mysterious — simply because we were both rebellious spirits — we liked each other immediately. I'm the type of woman who gets along well with men. Women tend to view me as their enemy.

Together we put out four issues of the magazine. When the opportunity arose to work in the building brigades, he was the first — though not the only — one to volunteer. What choice did he have? Our friendship deepened, and two years later I helped him furnish his new apartment. By this time, the Gusana had already left the country. Later, I helped him move to Miramar. We had a hilarious time figuring out where things should go, scraping and refinishing picture frames, reupholstering the furniture, planting ferns and orchids on the terrace. I was with him the day before he was arrested. I never heard from him again. Until today — I had just read the Gusana's letter (life is one big coincidence) — when he called me from Miami. And there I was still thinking he was in prison! He told me all about his adventures with the Japanese minister and the bonsai and all his long nights of solitary reflection on the Puntilla, with only the sea for company. And then those mysterious men who materialized out of nowhere, dragging their raft made of driftwood and old truck tires, with oars held together with rusty nails, and a tattered old sheet for a sail. They were loudly and nervously announcing that they were taking advantage of the full moon to go fishing. When they saw the Lynx they became even more afraid, thinking that he was a cop. They soon realized that he was just another outcast like themselves and invited him to join them. They asked whether he was staying or leaving. They assured him it was the chance of a lifetime. He shrugged his shoulders, made his way over the sharp-pointed rocks, and climbed on board. (See "Flashback" in the preceding chapter.)

❦

I remember it with total clarity: The telephone was ringing and ringing, and I was in the bathroom, making shampoo out of an aloe plant. Aloe works on just about anything, from dandruff to hemorrhoids. Whoever was calling was letting it ring so long I decided it had to be important. A ring, then a click, then a new tone. This meant the call was from overseas and that Big Brother was listening in.

"Gusanita! What's up? I just got your letter —"

"No, Yocandra. It's the Lynx." I lose control of my nerves, and the precious shampoo slips out of my hand and spills. "I'm . . ." I can hear a faint laugh on the other end and suspect he's trying to hold back the tears. ". . . here." The way he says "here," it sounds as if he's really "here" and not "there." "In Miami." I swear I almost peed in my pants.

"Listen, my Lynx, my Titan among men, I have everything to tell you, but I just can't."

The truth is, my throat is too tight to talk. I feel like a total shit. This is the first time that one of my angels has flown north — angel in the Rilkean sense that "every angel is a demon." I don't know what to do, what to give you, except some tiny drops of my heart's blood. How fast it has been beating these past few days — a sign, I'm sure — and yet I haven't the slightest clue why! The pall of death hangs heavily over Havana, City of the Winding Sheet, because it has lost one more illustrious citizen. Suddenly I have a fever. Sickness floods over me, violent and indescribable, but also completely logical. I feel as if I were the sole survivor in the country. Will you come back one day, radiant and without bitterness, the way angels return? (I begin to babble. My voice, like a derailed train, sounds husky and lyrical at the same time.) Take your time. Don't try to come back and be someone the minute you arrive. I'll offer up some little cakes to Elegguá, so that he'll protect you and prepare the way for you. Don't be seduced by that slut homesickness, the Cuban syndrome. Don't repress it either. Learn to take it in small doses. Endure it without letting it become obsessive, so that it serves as a spiritual nourishment, not a poison, and don't waste your time listening to old records. Don't stack them up in neat piles. Records are a farcical form of memory. We are near, very near. You are here, my Lynx, beneath my fingernails, entering me through every pore. No one inside or outside this miserable country will ever be able to tear you away from me, my friend, my brother, my lover, my child, *mon semblable,* to quote Jaime Gil de Biedma (quoting Baudelaire). Don't forget what's most important. Don't give in to the Cuban passion for stupid gossip. Don't drown in this separatist sea that you have crossed, the sea in which you saw so many other men die in panic. This sea unites us. We don't have to fight it. We have to become experts at avoiding the ocean's mortal traps. I know that to grope your way across is worse than death itself. From a point of high patriotic fervor we fall into utter decadence, playing with life as we used to play blindman's buff. I'm not being unfair. I know what despair and desperation mean. But I don't approve of battles lost in advance. Your flight was a miracle, though again I have to ask: how deep are the psychological scars? This sea, which belongs to us all, does it deserve all this blood we keep pouring into it? Will a path marked "Hope" one day appear unto us? I predict that you will be a brilliant block of stone in this bridge of human asphalt. An ugly image, but that's how I feel it. It'll be hard, but you'll succeed. What matters is not to lose your soul in trivialities. I know an exile doesn't even have the right to a headstone. Which earth will cover your body? The earth of wherever you are. Wherever you are, the earth is truly yours. You will overcome, despite the burden of being born Cuban. What wouldn't I give to change things! The ideal would be to live in an ideal country. Such is not our fate. We possess a country that is both poor and grand, that exhausts and delights, that loves us and hates us. A country obsessed with drawing wealth from poverty. We have all the complexity of being human and refusing to admit it, of being Cuban and trying to forget it. Where are the sonnets I dedicated to you, I wonder. I know I am raving like a madwoman. Let nothing break your will. Remember me, but if the thought of me makes you vulnerable, then forget me. I'll be the first to understand. I'll picture you in this imaginary place, waltzing or dancing the rumba, sweating or freezing, courageous or afraid. Agile, always be agile . . . in this imaginary place that belongs to so many of us, including those no longer among us, this place of hardship and grief: life.

"Yocandra, you're absolutely right. But I couldn't stand it any longer. Even if I were untouchable and homeless and carted off to prison — though allowed to keep my ration book — I'd had enough of the headlines in the morning papers. Every morning of my life they effaced my image in the pocket mirror the Gusana had given me. I couldn't stand the image they replaced me with:

Distribution of Food

The distribution of food corresponding to the present month will begin on the 28th (end of the month) in all retail outlets. For the following month, each person can expect to receive half a bar of soap. As for the normal quota of grain, 20 ounces of red beans will be distributed per capita in all stores, and the balance of the quota, namely six pounds, will be allotted according to instructions in the next announcement.

For the current month, the half liter of oil will be distributed in Central Havana and Cerro after being distributed in Playa, La Lisa, Marianao, Tenth of October, and Old Havana. Following which, distribution shall be made in San Miguel, Guanabacoa, Regla, and thereafter throughout the rest of the provinces until stock is depleted.

The program of the Under Ministry of Meat Products will be as follows:

There shall be three-quarters of a pound of meat per capita:

• Texturized ground meat: for the current month, the Boyeros section.

- Meat/soya mixture: Arroyo, Marianao, and Plaza. On the waiting list: Playa.

- Fricandel: the rest of Guanabacoa.

The Under Ministry for Supplementary Rations announces that there shall be a supplementary distribution of two pounds of beans throughout the provinces.

"I was on the verge of slitting my wrists with my comb, since I didn't own a knife. Whenever I smoked, I smoked supplementary tobacco. What kind of life is a life of supplements? When I was talking with a friend, the schedule of electrical power outages published daily in the only paper available, which consisted of just two pages, suddenly ran through my mind. My brain was slowly drying up. I can't even tell you what happened in prison, although from a psychological viewpoint it wasn't much different from life in the streets. That night on the shore, I wasn't even thinking of what the next second might bring. I hadn't the faintest idea what was going on in the present moment, for that matter. Suddenly those phony fishermen — who were about to set out on their pathetic raft — forced me into the notorious position between the rock and the hard place: to decide (one now realizes the importance of the verb 'to decide') to stay or to go? And so I left without even making up my mind, simply because I had nothing else to do. When we were far from the coast of Cuba — I don't know how many miles, about twenty or so, I would guess — we came upon the remains of some rafts. One of them contained the badly mutilated body of a young boy. On one of his dismembered arms was a wristwatch. Just then a school of giant sharks appeared out of nowhere, drawn by the smell of blood. One of the men, the oldest, told us in a low voice not to panic, but another man picked up an oar and started to swat at the nearest shark. I finally managed to grab hold of him and calm him down. Then the sea began to foam, and the wind shoved us forward. The prow of the little raft could no longer cut through the waves, which were eight or ten feet high. The fury of the swells capsized it. I don't know the precise moment when my traveling companions physically disappeared. Language and words are lost in a chaotic amnesia. Only silence remains. My muscles still hurt — the pain will be with me forever — from struggling so hard to keep from succumbing to the sea. I can only recount the story by evoking the inertia that remains embedded in my memory. Sea and blood. A great deal of both. I don't understand what happened to keep me alive — miraculously, as you put it — or that led to my being found and saved. Today, as I walk through the streets of southwest Miami at sundown, I have to pinch myself. Is this all a dream? Am I really alive? I would like to forget, but an energy welling from somewhere deep within me heightens my senses. Meticulously I go back over everything that happened and find no explanation, no possible solution. How is it possible to act with such impudence in the face of death? There were six of us, and all but two were between twenty and thirty years old. Their faces, which I lived with for only a few hours, will remain with me till the end of my days. How quickly and easily death links us to others for all eternity. There are those who maintain that people throw themselves into the sea over insignificant economic deprivations — can't get any blue jeans, can't find any chewing gum — but anyone who says that simply doesn't know Cuba, doesn't know the hunger and the terror the Cuban people have known; people who say that are those whose knowledge of the country is limited to the luxury hotels and the government protocol houses. I suffer every minute from my inability to describe my experience, but I have to believe I'll get used to it eventually. For one thing, I've stopped shaking, although I still break down and cry. The place where melancholy dwells must be enormous. I'll await whatever advice you have to give. I've met some old friends here, and there is a great feeling of solidarity among us, but none of them is you or the Gusana, nor any of the others who increasingly inhabit my dreams. Exile sharpens one's oneiric tendencies. I will have a number of job offers as soon as my status is legalized. For the moment, I'm working off the books and earning a decent living. I've been able to rent a small apartment. You want to know something? I looked for a place to live that would face your hexagonal attic apartment. Every morning I go out on the terrace and blow you a kiss. I hope that from now on you'll send kisses back.

"Are your parents still as crazy as ever? Send me the name of the sculptor. I may be able to track him down and give him the good news — that in his old Cuban home-stead, his house in the Vedado, lives a crazy old lady who venerates his Wifredo Lam and lives in the hope of return-ing it to him one day. As for me, nothing escapes me. A typical Pisces. I've visited a number of galleries as well as some bookstores, and I've been to the theater a number of times. Despite all the excellent Cuban actors and actresses who have emigrated, the level of the local theater is incred-ibly low. The cinema isn't much to brag about either. About the same as the Saturday-night fare over there, but in the form of documentaries. I keep exploring ways to persuade myself that I'm normal, that I can vault over the savage feeling of urgency that has always held me and ruined my plans and projects. That has always ruined my plans and projects. 'Lynx' rings in my ears like the word 'exile.' I have to admit that there are times when I yearn for my instability. Here I'm anonymous, and I can't stand anonymity. Back there I used to sleep under stairwells, but so long as the literary reviews appeared, I was being pub-lished — I know, censored! These are the kinds of con-tradictions that send you to the loony bin, or make you throw yourself into the sea or lock yourself in your room — turning the dead bolt twice to make sure and pretending the street doesn't exist. As you pointed out, one cannot land on a foreign shore and expect to be someone. I have to work hard. I mean really hard. Prove myself! Be faithful to this nickname — and what a scandalous nickname it is! — you and the Gusana stuck me with. Even here I can't rid myself of the compulsion to set goals. But I don't think I'll risk my life again. Starting over at age forty is a new kind of isolation. I'll treat it as a joke. Wish me luck! What more is there to say, except that our friendship is indissoluble. And now I must hang up, because this call is being routed through Canada and costing me two arms and a leg. I forget no one, I forget nothing."

❦

He hung up, and my phone went dead. Tomorrow I'll report it. State Security always screws up my line after I get a call from abroad. My God, it's seven o'clock! I find it hard to believe my conversation with the Lynx went on that long! I've got to get back to reality — bathe, make myself pretty. Tonight is the Night of the Nihilist. He told me not to cook because he was bringing a surprise for dinner. I somehow manage to detach myself from thoughts of the Lynx and plunge into the obscurity of the bathroom. The fluorescent bulb has been out for months, and I take my shower as best I can — by groping. What dress shall I wear? I must look like a scarecrow! Jesus, what a day! To put on my makeup in the dark and not end up looking like a Kabuki mask will take some doing. I'm using powder I've saved up since I was fifteen. Maybe the Nihilist will actually like my Daughter of Dracula look.

I should be thinking more about the Lynx, spending more time on his concerns and anxieties, and all the sorrows we share. I open my closet and look for my dress with the wine-colored little flowers. Not there. I go back into the bathroom and rummage in the dirty-clothes hamper. There it is. If I hadn't been so absentminded, I would have found time to wash it, dry it, and, in a flash, iron it — assuming there was any electricity — for it's made of a cloth that doesn't wrinkle. I'm going to wear my skirt and the black turtleneck. No. The goddess Oshún would be furious if she saw me wearing black! I think I'll wear the yellow blouse. No, child, you're far too thin. The yellow blouse would be a disaster. This is giving me a splitting headache and I've got no aspirin. And what if I wore nothing? What if I greeted him stark naked? A woman in love is fully capable of such an act. Whatever her age.

8

The Nights of
the Nihilist

"*I*T WOULD APPEAR that all Chapter Eights of Cuban literature are condemned to being pornographic."

Such will be the censor's report when he reads these pages. My personal censor — for every Cuban writer has his or her designated censor — will dictate those words to his secretary, who will type up the report on my novel, referring — to my credit — to Chapter Eight of José Lezama Lima's *Paradiso*, a masterpiece of world literature, which, needless to say, no censor has ever been able to read from start to finish. They fall asleep well before they reach the end, having understood nothing, literally nothing, not even why people say Chapter Eight is pornographic. But since they have to go on cataloguing it as such, no one will doubt the censors, who are incapable of telling the difference between the erotic and the pornographic. And that is why they are unable to understand that not only Chapter Eight but the entirety of *Paradiso* is erotic. From beginning to end, it is one of the most sensual novels in contemporary literature. After so much silence — so much censorship — for reasons more political than cultural, the censors have ended up being more Lezaman than the Pope.

I look at my watch. Already eight-thirty. Since seven-thirty I've been stark naked, bathed, perfumed, my hair flowing down over my shoulders. I even turned on the air conditioner. It seems they're not going to cut off the electricity tonight (they already cut it off this morning). I'm freezing, all curled up, waiting for the Nihilist, nipples erect, feet wrinkled, covered with goose bumps. In the background, Peter Frampton is singing "Show Me the Way."

The Nihilist is a film director, with several music videos to his credit. He has also directed one full-length feature, which he put together from raw stock that other, established directors had left on the cutting room floor. It took him seven years to make it, between prizes, interroga-

tions, imprisonment, confinements, dissidence, and rein-
tegration. Almost no one knows he's a director, because his
film was shown only once, during the Havana Film Festival.
It was never distributed commercially, because it's a post-
existentialist film, and we Cubans already lead a post-
existentialist existence. No need to inflict on the Cubans a
work that reflects a condition of which every Cuban is all
too painfully aware. Give them popular musicals, the more
mindless the better. Full of close-ups of buttocks brimming
with cellulite — here any model of sixteen is already
cellulite-ridden, for the flesh of even the youngest asses cannot resist the constant bombardment of beans — drooping
breasts, dyed hair, false eyelashes, and loads of cheerfulness
(the good old tropical kind), the kind tourists lap up, as
phony as possible. The Nihilist's music videos did not seem
to capture the public's fancy either. They all featured coun-
tercultural rock bands whose members were violent, un-
kempt, bare-chested and barefoot, and wore cut-offs that
looked as if they hadn't seen a laundry in years. Close-ups of
their shaggy hair filled the screen, their screams — crazed,
provocative screams — filled the sound track. In short, everything destined to disturb the peace of mind of the tourist
trade. As a result, the director, I mean the Nihilist, started
writing — with enormous hope and confidence and dedi-
cation, not to mention all the wild ideas young people have
when they undertake any artistic endeavor — a second scenario for a full-length feature. It's about three young Cubans who move from one end of the Malecón to the other.

They have a fight, and one of them jumps into the sea in an inner tube and heads for Miami, leaving the others behind, staring stupidly after him. In the end, the girl with whom the protagonist (the one who left for Miami) was in love takes off after him on a second inner tube and dies at sea. The script obviously has to be reworked, rewritten, rethought-out, remodeled, re-combined, readapted, relaunched. So it can be repressed. The Nihilist, who is nobody's fool, abandoned the project, reverted to silence, and retired to his lair, more paranoid than sad.

I met him at a young filmmakers festival, during the period when he was a self-declared dissident and the authorities were preventing him from finishing his first film. He made his way through the crowd as if he were invisible. I was seated on the floor on some cushions — not because it was chic, but because there were no chairs — next to the Lynx and the Gusana (who was too obsessed with the Lynx to see the Nihilist, otherwise she would surely have swiped him). With us were the Giant (who doesn't appear in this book because he's so big he'd take up every chapter), and the Pianist (who isn't in this book either, but he was the most clear-headed of us all, as well as being clairvoyant), and the Dentist (the most fun-loving member of the group). I can't remember if anyone else was there, and the reason I can't remember is that the Nihilist had managed to find some grass and some coke, very high quality, and before we knew it we were all sky-high.

I left ahead of the others. The Nihilist caught up with

me, and together we went looking for some more dope. None to be found. In Havana, you take what you can get and use it as soon as possible. We went up to my apartment, where we ground up all sorts of pills — Trifluoperazine, Valium, Diazepam, speed, and a number of barbiturates. We took a cigarette that we had bartered for in the street, mixed the powder we had just concocted with the tobacco, and smoked until well past dawn. We told each other the story of our lives, cross-eyed, euphoric, helpless with laughter, depressed out of our skulls, fantastically lucid. We smoked, we looked at each other, sometimes we touched. Nothing more. And then the Nihilist disappeared from my life.

Two years later, almost to the day, the Lynx came to see me. His face serious and flushed, he announced that he was going to help this young filmmaker whom the authorities seemed intent on persecuting. The Lynx said that the kid was on the verge of suicide and threatening to leave the country on an inner tube. I had no idea he was talking about the Nihilist. I was involved in a stupid fling with an actor, who went on to become a movie star. At noon there was a knock on my door. It was the Lynx and the Nihilist. Tucked under his arm, the Nihilist was carrying a video wrapped in an issue of *Granma*. By now I had become totally versed in video technology, and I set it up. The Nihilist said barely a word, but I could feel an enormous amount of energy emanating from him toward me, and vice versa. We sat down and watched his film.

"I don't see why the fuck they're calling this ideological deviationism!" was the Lynx's reaction, which was more passionate than professional. In any event, professionally speaking, there wasn't an iota of entertainment in the film. The Lynx called upon his *orishas*, the divinities Elegguá and Obbatalá, and thus cleansed, naked as the day he was born, did the Nihilist come back to the kingdom of this world. What could I do? My *orishas* steered me in the right direction too, and I did what goddesses — the most holy Oshún and the maternal Yemayá — always do in such cases: go on the offensive, body and soul.

❦

That night the Nihilist called me up. He let the phone ring twice, then hung up. I had spent the entire afternoon thinking of him. He called again, and on the third ring I picked up.

"Hi. You didn't say anything about my film. What did you think?"

"Come over and we'll talk about it. I don't want to discuss it on the phone. I have another video to show you. Do you know Jim Morrison?"

"He's one of my idols. Don't tell me you have *The Doors*! I've been trying to find it for centuries!"

"For centuries? I doubt that. The film only came out a few —"

"Just a manner of speaking. I'll be right over."

Ten minutes later, the doorbell rang. Sweat was pouring off him, for he had ridden over like a maniac on his bike across the Twenty-third Street, which is a minefield, especially for a bike without lights. His green eyes settled their gaze on my green eyes. His eyes are lighter; mine are the color of olives. It wouldn't have taken a mind reader to see that I was about to fall in love. Falling in love is like an obsession with me, and I had been going through one of the loneliest periods of my life because of the ephemeral company I'd been keeping. I needed someone intelligent, someone enigmatic. I needed the "love of my life." I needed to die for love, to live for love, to fall apart for love. To be in love with a guy who was in love with me. Someone who would understand that I'm not easy, that I'm half crazy and maybe even completely crazy. Today I love you, tomorrow I couldn't care less — the kind of exasperation few men are willing to accept. Not that I dreamed of having a good little husband. I was in search of the eternal lover. And though I may well be mistaken, I think I may have found him.

That night, like many others to come, our dinner consisted of rice and a fried egg. That was when eggs were still available on the free market. We did the dishes: two plates, two glasses, the frying pan, the pot, one fork (he didn't know how to eat with a fork), and a spoon. We lay down on the bed. Our bodies were rigid, but they hummed with an almost palpable energy. About halfway through the film, my foot accidentally touched his. He took this for a caress and plunged his perverse hand into my hair, just like Orlando's hand in the Virginia Woolf novel. I couldn't stand it any longer. I turned and kissed him on the lips. Right then I was sure I had found my man, for I recognized in his kiss the first kiss I had bestowed, many years before, on the curly-haired sculpture. He wiggled his tongue around the way you imagine adults do. We went on kissing for the rest of the film. We never managed to see that film all the way through. Whenever we put it on the VCR we could never get past the middle. Pavlov must have had a hand in it.

His kiss lasted as long as the film continued, but it didn't confine itself to my mouth. It descended, as if on an exploratory mission, slowly down to my neck, then, with little flicks of the tongue, moved from my chin to my nipples, where it lingered for several interminable minutes of pleasure. Then he slipped, even more slowly, from my breasts down my sides, and from there to my navel, where the tip of his tongue wreaked havoc. My stomach began to dance madly. After that, his long fingers parted my bush, to reveal, red and erect, my clitoris. He planted thereon a kiss that consecrated him, for all eternity, as a Nobel laureate of cunnilingus. His name should be etched in the *Guinness Book of Records*. I had seven orgasms or, better, I came seven times. When he finally took off his clothes, his body, which I could only compare to a Greek god's, left me open-mouthed: his shoulders were slightly wider than his hips, his smoky loins tanned to perfection by Indio, our national sun. He was thin-waisted, his buttocks perfect, smooth, the down from around his member surrounded his thighs. Symmetric well-muscled thighs, taut legs, solid ankles, feet extraordinarily elegant and well proportioned — a good sign — with the middle toe longer than the big toe, which bespeaks ancient Greece. His neck was perfectly proportioned too, neither too long nor too wide. Curly hair, his forehead sprinkled here and there with delicate locks. He had a straight, prominent nose. His lips were as dark and smooth as chocolate. Muscular arms, but not overly so, strong wrists, smooth, long hands — I've already mentioned them. How strange! He is an exquisite work of art, both outwardly and inwardly, for he is tender, patient, and peaceful. His voice has never risen. He is my lover, not my tyrant.

The Nihilist's prick — *¡Ayé!* blessed Lazarus, my Babalú — is the eighth wonder of the world. It could make him the head of one of the greatest fortunes of our century. Being endowed with a prick like that is like having millions in a Swiss bank. Before I forget, he has a beauty spot near his navel. And from that spot emerges, out of the pores, a fur so silky it's a dream to caress. And when your hand makes contact with the base of the member, your mouth waters and your lips foam. You just can't help it.

It's smooth. It measures six and a half inches at rest, twice that when standing at attention. Yet he has never hurt me. I don't know why. Maybe because I'm big inside myself, or because he's so masterful in the way he maneuvers it. And that includes when he's doing the backstitch — one stitch in front, one stitch in back, from vulva to anus and back again. The skin is like that of a newborn baby, and just beneath its surface lies a network of tiny red veins. You would think it's a garden of Black Princes, which is what they call red roses in Cuba. The prepuce is docile, sheathing and unsheathing as duty requires, like a Belle Époque shawl. To the touch, it has the warmth of royal jelly and a strength that would cure the worst tonsillitis. The shaft is solid, unperturbed by any unexpected movements of the earth and bolstered by the centuries, a true pillar of the Pantheon. The head I can only compare to the most advanced, most efficient computer software. It is precise and cerebral, and it persists until it has searched out every path to perfection. Like Picasso, his prick doesn't search, it finds. It is vibrant and delectable. It exudes an odor of skin washed with Mon Savon, that French soap concocted of ancient perfumes: essence of patchouli, jasmine, roses, goat's milk. Milk, my beloved's milk! If only our daily rations were at the same level! (What the aquatic Hernia is allotted every other day is pure unadulterated water — despite the fact that she calls it "concentrated milk." It has no trace of vitamins and is too insipid to leave a milk mustache. A doctor friend of mine diagnosed her as suffering from an ulcer, so she was able to obtain some real milk, and once in a while she gives me a little.) Milk, milk of my heart! This man's milk seems to spring forth as from a young Holstein, falling like manna from heaven, extraterrestrial sperm that gives you a mouthful of stars, shining brightly, interplanetary, transmitted by satellite. A cocktail of spermatozoa.

I'm shivering. I'm sure I'll catch the flu, and I haven't a single aspirin left in the house. The local drugstore won't have any either. No sooner do they come in — the aspirin — than they're gone. Despite the fact that they appear on the ration cards, the druggists sell them on the black market. I'm freezing, but I don't turn off the air conditioning because it's boiling outside and the Nihilist likes it to be cool when he makes love, imagining that we're in Europe and it's winter. I've already brushed my teeth four times. I have a theory that if you keep your mouth closed and don't talk to anyone for a long time, your breath goes bad. I breathe into my hands and smell them. No sign of halitosis that I can detect. Must be my imagination, or symptoms of the onset of schizophrenia, or the first signs of premature menopause.

I hear the sound of the key in the front door. He enters the room, my mad playboy of the tropical world, blinking his eyes because sweat is dripping into them. He chains his bicycle to the railing that protects the stairway entrance. He must be in a rage, because he hasn't even noticed that I'm nude. He carefully removes his backpack before closing the door to keep the cool air from escaping. Seated on the sofa, he mops his face with his red bandanna and tries to smooth the hair that's sticking to his cheeks.

Finally he lifts his eyes and looks over at me. His naked lady-in-waiting.

"I'm sorry, my love, but I'm a total wreck. My bike had a flat tire — and then it began to rain. Your shutters are closed, so you may not know that it was pouring out. I had to wait so long in line for pizza at the Piragua that my clothes had time to dry. The pizza delivery was late today. Incredibly late. You wouldn't believe how many people there were in line. If I had waited my turn, I would never have got any pizza. So I bought it from a scalper. You know what I had to pay? A hundred and twenty pesos! Sixty for each pizza! That's only thirty pesos less than my entire monthly salary. And the cheese isn't real cheese, it's some Chinese substitute. The people who work at the pizza place steal all the real cheese."

Dumbfounded, I watch him take two pieces of bread out of his knapsack, each more or less round, each a different size, both reeking of rancid cheese — I mean cheese substitute — and smeared with some reddish liquid that bears no relationship whatever to tomato sauce. We put them immediately into the oven in case the gas suddenly goes off. A minute later, we take them out of the oven and put them in two frying pans.

At last the Nihilist focuses on me, on my nudity, his playful eyes taking in each part of my body. He takes my hands and kisses them with his winged lips. He makes tender fun of my nakedness, settles his right cheek between my breasts, circles my waist with his arms; his hands take refuge on my loins. There's the smell of something burning. We eat the half-burned pizzas. We have won the battle of the beans. Eating pizza in Havana is like dining at the Tour d'Argent in Paris. Not only do you have to make a reservation to eat in a ramshackle pizza parlor, but you must be high up in the Militant Union pecking order. As for the McCastros, those cafeterias where they used to sell hamburgers made out of green soya ground up with mushrooms — green bird shit — they were victims of socialism. In other words, extinct. As for real hamburgers, when they do exist, you can only get them from the Committee for the Defense of the Revolution, which parcels them out exclusively to its own members.

The table is covered with an embroidered white tablecloth and napkins, a gift from the Gusana's grandmother to her parents on their forty-something wedding anniversary. Although the electricity is on, I light candles and put on a record of Gregorian chants. From his knapsack the Nihilist takes out the big surprise of the evening: a bottle of Beaujolais Nouveau. Real French wine! He got it from a salsa singer who travels abroad, in exchange for a 1930s armoire done in art deco, Creole style. He uncorks the bottle, and we drink to our love, sipping the wine daintily. His green eyes are locked on my olive-colored eyes. We devour the pizzas, our stomachs emitting indecent gargling sounds, being far from satisfied but somewhat placated by the Asian condiments. We polish off the bottle of wine, our heads not even beginning to spin. We realize that the wine by itself isn't strong enough to carry us away, so we begin to act as drunk as we'd hoped to get. We laugh till we cry, without knowing why. He takes off his clothes and chases me around the room, strewing furniture in his path, going the long way to make the game more exciting. He decides it is time to catch me, and he kisses me for a good ten minutes, until my tongue hurts, my gums ache, my chin cramps, my lips swell. He moves down toward my neck and begins a reprise. I pinch him because I don't like hickey marks. The pinch has an immediate effect. I can feel his member throbbing as his testicles stiffen and contract. My breasts grasp them tightly, and my tongue welcomes the regal head of the animal, the king of his pelvic jungle. I suck it until I can suck no more. He moves his hips back and forth, and the tip of his member penetrates beyond the uvula, and even then my mouth has taken in less than half. There are times when I have to hold on to it with all my might because I feel like throwing up. Vomiting and pleasure, retching and delightful nausea. My clitoris tightens, my moistened vagina opens wide. But he continues the assault on my throat.

When he is on the verge of ejaculating, he withdraws from my mouth in an incredible display of willpower. He goes into the bathroom and washes himself with cold water. He lays the bedspread down on the floor, and lying side by side, we caress each other lightly, tenderly. After a few minutes, his eloquent finger begins to massage my clit, as if he were masturbating a male member. My head bangs against the tile floor. He takes it gently in his hands and kisses me, first my forehead, then my eyelids, nose, cheeks, ears, mouth, and chin, his saliva flowing like a stream of tears over the oval of my face.

"Why don't we sit facing each other, you on top of me?"

A question that strikes me more as a suggestion.

I know he wants me to bury his sex in mine and move from one side to the other, from left to right and from right to left, churning my hips, embracing him with my eyes open, or bending forward so my breasts are within reach of his mouth and he can suck them to his heart's content. This is when I have my first orgasm. Slowly, I enjoy the pleasure centimeter by centimeter, my eyes capsizing into his, and the hair of his chest caressing my erect nipples.

An enormous moan topples me backward, my back arched. Taking advantage, he withdraws. In a state of fury, which astonishes me, he turns me over and pulls me to him. He spreads my legs and pulls them wide apart, and my nose finds itself buried in a silk cushion. His prick is resting between my buttocks, he squeezes them together and masturbates the way he sometimes does between my breasts. My anus suddenly yields to the pressure and I beg him to go on, but when the tip of his penis has barely penetrated, the pain is so excruciating I think I'm going to faint. That doesn't diminish the burning desire I experience when he takes me from behind, my hands helping him to spread my cheeks as he pushes little by little inside.

"Gently, gently," I beg.

The softness of my tone only inflames his desire more powerfully. The softer I beg, the more violent his thrusts. Suddenly his assault becomes bestial. There's no logical reason why, but my vagina begins to throb uncontrollably. He sticks his middle finger inside me and caresses his prick through the thin membrane. He's on the verge of coming, but holds back.

He collapses, with the full weight of his sculptural body upon me, and lies motionless, waiting for the effects of my orgasm to dissipate and for my desire to rekindle. My vaginal fluid, saplike, oozes down my thighs and legs, all the way to my knees. I've never known anything like it before. A primitive sensation stirs my nether lips; I need a man inside me, there, now! My skin is on fire. He rubs an ice cube in my armpits, my ankles, between my legs. He puts two ice cubes into my vagina. They melt virtually upon contact. He gets up and goes over to the little night table and pokes around in the drawer, licking his lips.

"What are you looking for?" I ask. I'm a little worried.

"Some Vicks and Tiger Balm," he says maliciously.

"What for? Do you think I have a cold?" I say, half joking, half fascinated.

"I've been told that the two together make an incredible lubricant."

"You're out of your mind. Let's give it a try."

He empties half of the tube of Vicks into my cunt. He dips the head of his member into the jar of Tiger Balm. I can't help laughing at the idea that he's trying to cure a different kind of headache. My sex begins to feel like a hot-air balloon, a dirigible, and the walls of my vagina are so tight they feel as if they're stuck together. He kisses me, his member tickling my bush. I come for the third time. I can't help it. It's at this point, breathless and mentholated, that he penetrates me up to the navel. My vagina gasps for air, and my sex spits fire, goes quiescent, bursts into flames again — all the result of the two ointments, the Vicks and the Tiger Balm, acting in concert. It's as if someone had set a full box of matches on fire inside me, and each and every match was an orgasm that weakened my senses and made me more receptive to pleasure. I lose count. I have no idea how many times I've come. Countless. I'm on the verge of losing consciousness, when he presses his lips against mine and kisses me, long and lovingly. A spasm, emanating from our centers of gravity, seizes us both. Seconds later, his sperm floods into my vagina. I have phantasmagorical visions. Thus ends our Nine and a Half Weeks. All we've done is replace the strawberries, the cherries, the champagne, and the whipped cream with ointments to lessen the pain.

"I love you, light of my life, I love you I love you I love you," he goes on repeating, insatiable.

"I love you too," I respond, barely able to speak.

It seems so lame to repeat words that have already been said so many times. Clichés and banalities. But we still have to say them. It is an absolute necessity. The words of love that ring most true are the least original.

"I'd really love to have a daughter with you."

"This isn't the time for such craziness. I'd give anything to be sterile. But I have to be careful. I get pregnant just smelling sperm."

I yawn, having said the opposite of what I feel. But what's the point of dreaming?

"It wouldn't be crazy. It would be wonderful." He curls up into a fetal position. "This afternoon, when I was in line waiting for pizza, I had a great idea for a film. I visualized it scene by scene, in my head. I have to write the scenario. . . . I have to shoot the story. . . ."

I gently massage his temples. The whole place reeks of eucalyptus. His eyelids close, his breathing deepens. Why is it that after lovemaking, the men always fall asleep first? No sooner has that thought gone through my mind than his eyes half open:

"I'm not asleep. I'm thinking."

"About what?"

"About you, silly, about you."

His eyelids flutter, his facial muscles relax, and, very softly, he begins to snore. Again he shifts position, stretching his arms above his head. The impertinence of my gaze wakes him up.

"And about the film I'm going to make. I'm also thinking about the film I want to make."

I don't want to sadden him by telling him that the

Lynx called, or ruin his night by telling him about the letter from the Gusana. We have enough problems coping with our pitiful illusions and our truncated plans. Better to let him dream about his film, to leave his obsessions intact. Poor boy, maybe he's already dreaming he's onstage, accepting an Oscar from Jane Campion or Peter Greenaway. He's a phenomenal Nihilist, and it's not for me to destroy that magic. I've never for a moment regretted any of our nights together.

9

And to Think I Used to Put Him on a Pedestal!

I WAKE UP BECAUSE SOMEONE is leaning on my doorbell. I feel as if we've been asleep for hours, but the alarm clock shows that it's only been thirty minutes. The Nihilist's skin is still tingling. We throw on some clothes in a hurry. No one ever comes up here unannounced, and we certainly weren't expecting anyone. I'm scrupulous about which days I devote to the Traitor and which I devote to the Nihilist. I open the door. The Traitor, of course. He kisses me decorously on the cheek, to keep the Nihilist from becoming suspicious. The Traitor is fully aware of my relationship with the young man and accepts it. He knows that it's pure vendetta. The Nihilist is also aware that I continue to see my first husband, but he thinks I do it out of charity, since the man's a psycho. I lie to them both, explaining that on the two nights a week they can't see me it's because I'm taking French lessons with Madame Lénormand, a professor who gives private lessons at her house in the boondocks. I tell them — a complete lie — that I'm self-disciplining myself and don't want to lose my accent or my vocabulary. Both believe me, or at least pretend to. The Traitor gives me a polite peck on the other cheek.

"You're hot," he says bluntly. "Do you have a fever?"

"No, we just finished fucking," I say with utter cynicism.

"Ah. Well, at least I didn't arrive while you were still at it. Listen, Yocandra, I'm really sorry, but I borrowed that little book by the French postmodernist philosopher, you know the one, Jean-François Lyotard, and I have to finish reading it because they want it back tomorrow morning. The electricity's been cut off at the house, and I don't even have a used candle —"

"All right, all right. Come in. Go out on the balcony. By the way, I'd like you to meet the Nihilist."

It was in this way that the Nihilist first learned the nickname I'd given him. He was surprised, but I could see that he was pleased.

"And you," he said, "must be the Traitor," letting the name slip out before I could stop him.

"The Traitor? First I've heard of it. So that's what Yocandrita calls me! Because I'm sure it's your idea — right, Yocandrita?" I can tell that he's furious, but he's feigning indifference. "What would you like to cut off first, the head or the tail?"

"Don't call me Yocandrita. You know how much I hate diminutives. And yes, it was my idea. So what? Wasn't it your idea, way back in another life, to make fun of my real name?"

"Me make fun of you? I have always been, and continue to be, completely respectful toward you."

Restraining myself, I leave them both in the living room, staring at one another, each jealous of the other. I go into the bathroom, sit down on the commode, and savor the ecstasy of my emptying bladder. Through the air shaft, I can hear them talking.

"Have you ever heard anything so despicable, so libelous? A traitor? Me? Me, a traitor! Why? Why have I deserved such a name?"

The Nihilist shrugs his shoulders as if he hasn't the faintest idea and goes to the kitchen to brew up a little jasmine tea — Lipton tea from a friend in Mexico. He takes advantage of the noise made by the boiling water to avoid listening to the rest of the Traitor's tirade. The Traitor rambles on incoherently. From my perch, I can actually see them both, at a slant through the windows, one of which overlooks the kitchen, the other the living room — the omniscient narrator.

"I don't deserve that nickname. I really don't. By the way, I'm sure you know who I am. I'm her first husband, the one who taught her everything she knows. And I mean *everything* —"

"You're exaggerating, man," the Nihilist broke in. "A few others have taught her some things. Not to mention what she's learned on her own. She's very bright. Maybe we owe her a lot too."

"I don't owe her a thing. Not a damn thing. I've always been brilliant myself. Did she tell you what I do?" the Traitor asked, clearly ill at ease.

The Nihilist nodded. "Yeah. She said you're a philosopher."

"*And* a novelist. Tell me something: doesn't it bother you that she's dubbed you the Nihilist?"

"Well . . . yes and no. I find it beautiful, poetic, a little faggy. I don't know whether I deserve it or not. Maybe she calls me that to avoid calling me Shithead."

The Traitor doubles over with laughter. Coughs. His voice deserts him and his chest produces a sickly whistling sound. He fumbles in his pockets, still roaring with laughter, and pulls out a pack of cigarettes, the Cuban national brand with a green logo, the kind the ration card limits to those over thirty-five. He lights up and exhales, creating a curtain of smoke between him and the young man.

I finish peeing I don't know how many quarts, pull

the chain, and reappear as if I had just dropped in unexpectedly.

"Didn't you come here to read?" A cheap shot to put him on the defensive.

"Yes, but . . . I was in deep conversation with the . . . Nihilist," he replies, stressing the nickname. He goes off again into gales of laughter, then looks serious again, probably as a result of my dark look. "We were intrigued about the origin of our respective nicknames."

We drink our tea. I stretch out on the sofa, my feet propped up on a pillow. I keep my eyes lowered. Bitter experience as a wife has taught me not to lose all discretion. Explaining to the Traitor why I baptized him thus would bring old grudges to the surface and reopen old wounds. It would be telling him what I really thought of him, something I'd never been able to do, not even when I was alone in front of a mirror. Nonetheless, my lips start moving mechanically.

"Don't think I still resent all the times you cheated on me. They're of no importance, to me or to anyone else. And don't think I'm still under your spell or that I want you to feel indebted to me. What I do, I do out of pure humanity. Because revenge is human. I could have thrown you out tonight, but I asked you to stay. You asked about my name for you, but don't delude yourself. There's nothing personal about it. And it's not because you betrayed me over and over again. I know you've changed your politics. You used to be an out-and-out ass-kisser. Now you go out of your way to avoid the slightest compromise with the regime. I'm not stupid. I can see that you're carefully constructing a file for yourself as a future dissident, to save your skin in the event things go the other way. But that's not the reason I called you the Traitor either. You really have no idea? Ever look in the mirror? When are you going to stop betraying yourself? When are you going to begin being honest with yourself? When are you going to stop telling people that you're writing a book? What you're really doing is punishment, as if you were a naughty schoolboy. Six hundred pages of the same line copied over and over again: 'I'm a writer. Everyone is persecuting me and I can't write. I'm a writer.' Or whatever it is you say. You cultivate opposites. You live in betrayal. You're betraying yourself. You have a need to betray everything, even the little things in life. Once, you went to have a tooth pulled — a healthy tooth — to convince yourself you wouldn't be able to work for months. Do you remember? Why do you go on screwing up your whole life on purpose? If I agreed not to break off all relations with you, if I agreed to keep on seeing you, it was because I wanted revenge. I also think I'm helping you. Aside from anything else, I'm giving you a chance to reassess things, before you finally make up your mind to commit suicide. Because you're an obvious candidate for slitting your wrists. Assuming you can lay your hands on a razor blade, of course. Or poisoning yourself with pills — though I defy you to find a drugstore that has any pills. There's always the sea, the exit of last resort. You'd probably inspire greater pity, which you so sorely need, if you drowned yourself. You're addicted to pity, just like a druggie. When I wanted to rebaptize you, I hesitated for a long time. It came down to two possibilities: the Victim or the Traitor. I chose the latter because it's broader. Also, when you come right down to it, a traitor is always a victim. It's finished. I don't even hate you anymore. I could spend the rest of the night insulting you, but I'll refrain. If you had the slightest shred of self-respect left, you'd leave. If you don't, stay. You'll always have a refuge here. But under the following condition: the dictatorship is over."

"And *your* dictatorship is just beginning?" he asked sarcastically, without the slightest show of embarrassment.

My hand took off of its own accord and applauded his face. Slap! Slap! Slap! Three slaps across the face, just like in the movies.

Up to now the Nihilist had watched us silently, shaking visibly, but just as my hand was about to administer a fourth slap to the impertinent face of the Traitor, the Nihilist caught it in midair.

"Please, if you love me, I beg you not to make me see this. You should have worked this out between you ages ago."

The Traitor calmly lights a cigarette, the muscles of his reddened face trembling, the mark of my five fingers forming a lovely abstract drawing on his skin. He takes his book and goes out onto the balcony to read the pages in

which — according to him — Jean-François Lyotard re-
tracts his entire opus. I'm absolutely sure he'll go on seeing
me, because he's a shameless addict and a complete bas-
tard. The Nihilist has his head buried in his hands. To
make him lift his eyes and look at me, I ask:

"Do you need to know why I baptized you the Nihilist? Does that intrigue you?"

"The only person it ought to intrigue is you. I
thought you were sincere with me. All I need is love. It's as
simple as that. I don't want to hurt anyone, least of all
you —" And with that he breaks off his insipid but heart-
felt speech.

My eyes are almost bleeding tears. I open them, and
huge drops of the salty liquid unglue my eyelids. I feel as if
I'm dying. I *am* dying. Too many things are happening at
once. Yet it seems as if nothing is happening, as if I've been
doing the same thing since I was born: sulking, exploding,
sobbing. Sulking, exploding, sobbing. My days of passivity
are over. Melancholy is my revolt, the strike I'm calling to
declare the independence of my own sadness and the
collective sadness, to reduce my salaried anxiety, paid for
with the wages of duty. As if those wages could buy, for
example, sugar or gasoline. I was born owing a transcendental debt. I should have remained faithful to my
ancestors. I should have been faithful to my *patria*. I
should have been faithful to my school. I should have been
faithful to the mass organizations, and to others as well. I
should have been faithful to national symbols. I should

have been faithful to my *compañeros,* my comrades (the word "friend" has been eliminated). I should have been faithful to my husband — I mean my "comrade-spouse." I should have been faithful to everything faithful to me. Faithful to a fault, or by default. Beloved paternalists, see how faithfulness is killing me. Faithless, I cry, and it is the cowardly proof of my courage. To know that I'm crying because I believe in nothing. Not even in you, Nihilist, who watch me dry-eyed, not lifting a finger to stem my hysteria. All he's doing is bobbing his foot up and down, as if he were using an old Singer sewing machine. I cry because everything is suddenly happening to me — to whom nothing ever happens, who's always doing the same thing: pedaling away to get lost in my thoughts. There are times when I think I could die, when I think that every- thing that was supposed to happen to me has happened already, so quickly that I wasn't even aware of it. The truth is, the only two things I own in the world are my bicycle and my mind. Today my whole life suddenly came tum- bling down around me: my childhood, my parents, the Gusana, the Lynx, the Traitor, the Nihilist, the office, the sea . . . the country. How can I turn things back so that I can have different parents, different friends, different loves, different work, a different sea . . . a different coun- try? Or none at all. How can I cease being me? Me with my *nada,* my trifles, my pathetic daily droppings. To deceive no one, least of all myself, I should clean all this crap out of my head and devote myself to the fictitious me. Pull out the business cards reserved for my other life: I, the editor in chief of a prestigious literary review. I go to the general meetings as well as the ones reserved for top executives, and I'm invited to all the embassy receptions. I keep my mouth shut, because if you keep your mouth shut mosquitoes can't get in. My comrade ambassadors treat me to delicious dinners and endless glasses of champagne. The champagne flows, for it loosens the tongue, and they want you to talk, talk about everything you know and everything you don't know. At least they're more generous than those on the other side, the ones who say that if you spill your guts and turn in your mother, your corpse will be turned over to your family. But that's not my life! That's not me! Yet that's how you live. That's how you act. It's the spitting image of you, your portrait. *Coño*, don't you see that I'm losing the most heroic part of myself, of life itself, when I join the ranks of the happy few, the smug, the battalions of people with medals on their chests, those who give their lives for the latest militant slogan, however hollow. Don't you see I'm losing my friends? They've left, or they're planning to leave, and I can hardly say their names in a normal tone of voice. I have to pretend I'm not happy when I hear that they're alive and well, that they have found work, that they've managed to save a little money and may be planning to come back for a visit. But they no longer live here. We're no longer together day in, day out. We can't say to one another whenever we feel like it, "Let's go over to So-and-so's house," because So-and-so, Such-and-such, and What's-his-name have all gone to Miami; or to Mexico, so that a coyote can sneak them across the border; or to Spain, where they're treated like untouchables; or to France, to be enslaved and bombarded with more useless politics. Don't you see, you paternalistic studs, how you're murdering all my friends? And my family? What a band of loonies they've become. They don't even know any longer they're part of the human race. All they know is they belong to the Party, which for them is the summit of everything, higher than being human.

"Can you tell me why you're crying?" he finally asks in a faint voice.

"I don't know. I have no idea. There are days when I cry and cry until I drop from exhaustion. The next day I remember nothing. It's like getting drunk."

"Do you want me to leave? I can come back tomorrow."

"No! Please don't go. Don't leave me alone."

I screw my eyes up tight because of the tears. I look a little like Ochín, the woman in the Japanese soap opera shown on Tuesdays and Thursdays. Ochín, the humble servant, eating plain rice with a spoon. The Nihilist takes his bandanna out of his trouser pocket and wipes my face. For some reason, this makes me sad again, and my tears soak his handkerchief. He can't figure out what to do to take my mind off whatever is bothering me, and he paces back and forth across the room. He notices the Traitor, who is stretched out in the hammock on the balcony, reading. And since the Nihilist is only human, he's fed up with seeing me blow my nose. He makes no special effort to show that he's different. If only he were a demigod, a demisavior, because the gods . . . the gods! How arrogant they've become with their poor creations. The Nihilist goes into the bedroom, opens the dresser, takes out the chessboard, and sets up the pieces.

After two hours of playing chess by himself, the Nihilist notices that the Traitor has closed his book. He's finally finished.

"So. Anything new in postmodernism?"

"Nothing new under the sun. Theories, theories, and more theories, each subtler than the one before. To understand them, you have to live in industrialized cities. We're like the beasts in the field, waiting, waiting, waiting, whether for a carnival float or a hearse. Like the lyrics in that Willy Chirino song, 'Ya viene llegando' — 'It's the beginning of the end.' "

They cackle like two bullies. The Nihilist shows him the black chess pieces and invites him to play. The Traitor accepts. Is there a bet? Yes, the winner will get to kiss me. What a pair of idiots! They're playing chess, and you'd think they were playing spin the bottle. My mind goes blank, alternately filling and emptying. I stare at their backs, their furrowed brows, their slicked-back hair, as they run their tense hands nervously through it — the way cowboys do in the movies — and their serious expressions. You'd think we were watching Karpov and Kasparov at the height of their powers. The Nihilist and the Traitor are wasting their brain cells for nothing, to kill time until dawn. Why are they so desperate to win? Come on, the prize is only my lips, my muzzled mouth.

While they play chess, I escape back into my hexagonal refuge, the room in which three windows show the sea in three different moods. Through the right window the waves roll in, huge, foaming, furious. Through the middle window, the sea is like a lake, bright blue, alive with the surrealistic glitter of the tropical sun. And through the left window the sea is black, with stars floating on its swells. All three windows reflect both the moon and the sun, night falling and day breaking in quick succession, flickering light and dark like an old film clip.

"Grunt, grunt, grunt." The pig that the neighbors across the hall are fattening up in their bathtub.

"Gobble, gobble, gobble." The turkey that belongs to the people on the floor below, answering the call of the pig from the depths of the closet in which they keep him.

From the floor above, the goat bleats, answering the turkey. They keep the goat tied up on the tiny balcony.

"Cock-a-doodle-doo, cock-a-doodle-doo, cock-a-doodle-doo." The rooster is waking up the whole neighborhood. The rooster in the lobby — not the one in the kitchen — with its cracked call. He has never adjusted to the building's schedule or the inhabitants' complaints. The animals are all being raised in apartments and the people relegated to asylums. People go in the asylums as Communists and come out as monks.

"Cock-a-doodle-doo!" The rooster's crow fills me with optimism. Suddenly a hyperrealist sun shines through the windows. It's another day. The rooster gives me strength. Its song makes more sense than the songs they play for the annual "Best New Popular Song" prize in the Spanish-speaking countries. From Cuba to Valencia, we count the years from one competition to the next. Who'll get it this year? People resort to reading entrails to try and guess the winner. Why not enter the rooster's song?

I can hear the sound of drums. A ceremony in honor of Changó. So early, and already it's as hot as a war zone. The sun beats down mercilessly. A crushing blow, a hatchet hanging over my neck. Blessed Saint Bárbara, *viva* Changó! Now the people are beating a drum for the *orishas* the way they used to sing at the beginning of classes, or on the Friday celebrations honoring the liberation of Vietnam. Who knows? Maybe all that is linked together in some mysterious way. Everything connects. Black blood flows in my veins, no question about it. As soon as I hear the sound of drums, my heart starts to beat faster, my soul fills with indescribable joy. My head is trapped between distant cries and songs of lamentation. Prayers to religion? Prayers to the *nada?*

The two men are still bent over their chessboard, with its queens and kings, its rooks and knights. How appropriately man has modeled the games he plays in his image! In his image and likeness! A cloud of flies and mosquitoes invades the kitchen. The garbage is rotting. I grab the bag and take it down to the street. Time to toss out this little package of disgusting *nada*.

As usual, the garbage cans are filled to overflowing. In the street, five or six old ladies are sifting through the foul-smelling refuse. The oldest among them suddenly remarks in an unrepentant tone:

"And to think I used to put him on a pedestal!"

What was that she just said? A crowd of shrews armed with sticks and poles suddenly appears from behind a row of nearby columns and begins to circle the old woman in a threatening manner.

"Who was it you used to put on a pedestal?" asks the most aggressive woman in the bunch.

"You know who . . . no one . . . it's just talk."

"Is that right? Just talk? Listen to me, you crone, you old bat, you bag of bones, you sewer rat. You'd better watch what you say, or we'll beat you to a pulp."

The old lady beats a hasty retreat, whistling the "Internationale" to efface any trace of suspicion or misunderstanding. As soon as the women think we'd all left, this band of militant she-women, who look for all the world like socialist-realist statues, start rooting around in our bags of garbage. Not for food. For evidence. Each scrap of paper will be examined, discussed, added to our personal files. They say that even our toilet paper — back issues of

Granma — are filed away after being meticulously analyzed to dissect our ideology. Apparently our politics can be determined from our excrement. Here any kind of repressive shit job is much sought after. If you doubt my word, just look at the RRB — the Rapid Response Brigade. They get chicken for lunch, sandwiches and Coppelia's chocolate ice cream for afternoon snacks, and chicken for dinner. No wonder the whole starving country wants to join the ranks of the RRB. They live in dormitories overlooking the waterfront. They don't do a lick of work. All they do is make sure that the people don't get out of line, and beat the hell out of them if they do. The more vicious they are, the more chicken they get.

I walk back upstairs slowly. With each step upward I take, my fear grows. I'm afraid, I admit it, and my fear is growing. This is the first time I've felt afraid, irrationally afraid. I expect a knife in my back. I'm afraid of being poisoned, or scorched by a flamethrower, or clubbed on the back of the head. Nothing happens. Nothing direct. Nothing I can see or feel. I open the gate. I walk into the apartment and am greeted by the symphonic sound of snoring. The Traitor and the Nihilist are fast asleep in my bedroom. The chessboard is empty, the pieces scattered all over the floor. As far as I can tell, neither won. Except sleep. The pills I slipped into their tea did their job.

In my hexagonal cell, I take a deep breath, inhaling the smell of barley-laced coffee. Day breaks steadily. The sun beats down, yet a cool breeze ruffles my hair. The sea is

bluer than blue, and above it there floats a garden of sun-
flowers, tulips, oleanders, everlastings, hibiscus, orchids,
jasmine, daisies, and every other flower in creation. The sky
is pure, less sparkling than the sea. How beautiful, how
utterly beautiful, this harmony of light and color. I've never
seen anything like it. But are they flowers or coffins? Is this
a garden or a cemetery? I want a garden. I need a garden.
How proud I am to be Cuban! How terrified I am to be
Cuban! Let my eyes see clearly! Are those natural lights or
searchlights? It's a garden. I'm sure it's a garden. The Fatherland or Death! Stop the bullshit! Oh, sure, it's wonderful to be living this experiment in revolution! Even when
you remember that it's killing us all off little by little. Each
time we blink our eyes and cease to see, and to hear. Listen:
a supersong, a superlife. Let us make a revolution greater
than ourselves, one so great it will collapse under its own
weight. I'm sitting in front of a notebook filled with lined
pages, waking my brain. I take a sip of coffee, which is
wonderful — what am I saying? — which is dreadful. I
should have put more sugar in it. I'm casting my eyes about
at every object around me, however small, to keep from
thinking. To keep from getting into something I may not be
able to pull off: describing the *nada* that is my everything.
But over there in Madrid, the Gusana, poor child, wants
me to send her a best-seller. What if I disappoint her? And
the Lynx is no longer around to tell me it's a work of pure
genius and must be published at whatever cost, even if it
means dying for it. I know it won't be a work of genius. I

know my limits. I'm the linguistic product of the worst teachers on the face of the earth. I don't overestimate myself. I have to keep myself from writing long sentences because I'm a stringer together of unnecessary words. I'm no champion when it comes to verb tense either. Far from it. No one needs to tell me I should have read a lot more of Lezama and Proust than I did. I kiss the middle window and know that the Lynx is doing the same thing on the other side. We are encircled by the same ocean.

I invoke my *orishas:* Give me strength! Maybe I should go brush my teeth, comb my hair, change my dress. Why am I so ceremonial? I'm afraid, *coño*. It's true. That's why I bounce around so much. That's why I see miles and miles of rafts filled with corpses. That's why I'm more terrified than anyone on the face of the earth. That's why I chatter and chatter, then chatter some more. To keep me from beginning. To keep me from starting a sentence. To censor my own words. Some words are madwomen, some are prostitutes, some are fairies, some are goddesses, and all pushing and shoving their way from the ink of the pen I hold tightly between my fingers. Because I have had friends who have died, others who have fled, still others who have remained. They are all inside me. Inside the words. I no longer know if I have written them. Or if they have written me:

"She comes from an island that had wanted to build paradise. . . ."

Translator's Note

This novel contains a number of references and allusions particular to Cuba and to the dialect of Spanish spoken there. The following list may interest readers.

Page v. *Periodo especial.* The phrase, first used by Castro, refers to the "Special Period" of severe financial difficulties Cuba has experienced since the collapse of its Soviet patron in 1990.

Page 1. *"Morir por la patria es vivir,"* a line from the Cuban national anthem, translates roughly as "To die for one's country is to live."

Page 15. *Picadillo de soya,* made of soya and ground beef, is a staple of the Cuban diet.

Page 17. *Agricultural school—escuela al campo*—is essentially a work camp at which students who have "volunteered" help to meet agricultural quotas.

Page 26. *26th of July flag.* July 26 is a holiday, commemorating the attack on the Moncada garrison in Santiago (July 26, 1953) by Fidel Castro and his guerrilla forces.

Page 28. *Malecón*, Havana's most popular promenade, borders the sea and is the place to be "seen." It is here that many of the *jineteras*, part-time hustlers mentioned several times in the text, can be found.

Page 36. *García Márquez*, the Colombian novelist, is a confidant of Castro's. *Régis Debray* is a French writer and journalist who once went in search of Che Guevara. *Alejo Carpentier* is one of Cuba's best-known novelists and the author of *The Chase*.

Page 44–45. *Patrick Süskind's* Perfume: Castro once said that this German novel was his favorite, and, translated, it became a huge hit in Cuba. *Lezama Lima*: Cuba's foremost poet and essayist, José Lezama Lima is most famous for his novel *Paradiso*, which is mentioned on page 117. He died in 1976.

Page 54. *Yemayá* is a deity in Santería, a widely popular Cuban religion that is made up of a blend of West African and Catholic influences. Other deities invoked by a number of characters throughout the text are Elegguá, Oshún, Changó, Babalú, and Obbatalá. See *orishas*, page 122.

Page 64. *Committee for the Defense of the Revolution*, or *CDR*, refers to the neighborhood societies formed throughout Cuba to monitor anti-revolutionary activities and behavior.

Page 64. *Wifredo Lam* was Cuba's most prominent modern painter. He studied with Picasso and was deeply influenced by cubism.

Page 93. *Microbrigadista*, or "microbrigade worker," is a volunteer (here, female) who helps build housing from materials provided by the government and who for her efforts will be rewarded with a house of her own. These houses tend to look uniform, the Cuban equivalent of a home in suburbia.

Page 152. *RRB*, or "Rapid Response Brigades," are government-sponsored vigilantes—*Brigadas de Repuesta Rapida*—who maintain order and work with the CDR.